It was all arrange[illegible], wit and charm, romance in the air. . . there was no telling where it could lead. Max Ramsay rubbed his hands together in gleeful anticipation. Ah yes – romance. Max was a very happy man.

He and Laura would have the house to themselves. The kids would be out, and Madge had taken him up on his offer of a ticket to the movies. Dinner, too – there had been some hard bargaining. A small snag had arisen when she flatly refused to cook the dinner for them, but then, after tackling the problem head on, he had come up with his great idea. 'I know,' he had exclaimed brightly. 'I'll ring one of those gourmet home delivery places. They only charge about sixty bucks for two and you get three courses.' It was a simple solution to the problem. A weight had been lifted from his mind.

Also by Carl Ruhen and available in Star Books

SONS AND DAUGHTERS 1
SONS AND DAUGHTERS 2
SONS AND DAUGHTERS 3
SONS AND DAUGHTERS 4
SONS AND DAUGHTERS 5
SONS AND DAUGHTERS 6
SONS AND DAUGHTERS 7

NEIGHBOURS 1
NEIGHBOURS 2
NEIGHBOURS 3

YOUNG DOCTORS 1

NEIGHBOURS 4

Carl Ruhen

From an orignal concept by Reg Watson and based on the scripts of Ginny Lowndes, Cheredith Mok, Sally Webb, Roger Moulton, David Phillips, Peter Connah, Reg Watson, Adrian van den Bok, John Upton, Ray Harding, Phillip Ryall, Nicholas Langton, Christine Schofield, Christine McCourt, Penny Fraser, Jill James, Rick Maier, Ysabelle Dean, John Linton, Dave Worthington, Ray Kolle, Greg Stevens, Lois Booton, Christine Stanton, Bill Searle, Greg Millin, Betty Quin.

A STAR BOOK
published by
the Paperback Division of
W.H. ALLEN & Co Plc

A Star Book
Published in 1988
by the Paperback Division of
W. H. Allen & Co. Plc
44 Hill Street, London W1X 8LB

Reprinted 1988

Printed and bound in Great Britain by
Cox & Wyman Ltd, Reading, Berkshire

ISBN 0 352 32284 5

One

In many ways it would have been easier if Des were in love with Andrea. He wasn't, and that made it difficult. But Bradley was his son. Andrea was the boy's mother. He owed it to both of them – as he tried to explain to Eileen.

'Look, Mum, can you imagine what it feels like for *any* father to be suddenly confronted by the fact that he has a son he knew nothing about?' Des looked steadily at his mother who, flushed and angry, was still trying to come to terms with the fact that she was now, suddenly, a grandmother. 'You said it yourself – how you had to bring me up single-handedly.' He sighed. He could see he wasn't getting through to her – he hardly ever could – and he wondered, as he had wondered so many times before, why he bothered. 'Well, for the last ten years it was the same for Andrea.'

For ten years, Andrea had lived over there in Perth, bringing up his son single-handedly, until suddenly the two of them had arrived on his doorstep. 'Then why did she have to wait ten years?' Eileen Clarke looked sourly at Andrea. 'Why didn't you get in touch with Desmond earlier?'

There was no love lost between the two women. Eileen had never liked Andrea and had done everything she could to put an end to her relationship with Des. 'Well... I was ashamed... Yes,' Andrea replied, 'and confused. I knew how much you were against me going out with Des.' She smiled a little wanly. 'So I did what any girl in that situation would do – I told my parents, and they stood by me. But as Bradley gets older it's becoming quite clear that he needs a father– *his* father. And Des...' She gave Des a quick, grateful smile... 'Well, he's been quite wonderful.'

Eileen had been outraged when she arrived at the house and found Andrea and the boy already installed. Words had been exchanged. The truth had come out, Eileen had refused to believe it – and she had telephoned Des at the bank, asking him to come home immediately. Now she sighed heavily. 'Well, I suppose if you *are* convinced he is your son,' she said to Des, 'then we must put a brave face on it and... she straightened in her chair... 'shoulder our responsibilities.'

'*You* don't have to do anything,' Des said sharply. 'It's none of your business. Bradley is *my* responsibility. And I'm going to make it up to him.' He glanced across at Andrea. 'And Andrea. For those lost years.' He stood up and moved across to the door before his mother had a chance to protest.

That night, when Bradley went to bed, Des stayed with him in his room until he had fallen asleep. It was a new and quite strange sensation for him to sit on the edge of the bed, talking quietly with his son, slowly coming to know him. He asked him what his school in Western Australia had been like.

'It was good. They taught me lots – except one thing.'

'What was that?'

'Girls.'

'Girls, eh?' Des thought of the paternal duties that lay ahead of him. 'The birds and the bees – I suppose you know about them?'

'I know about them.' Bradley stared earnestly up at him from the pillow.

'Girls, I mean, as real people.'

Bradley nodded. 'Yeah, sure.'

It would be just a matter of gaining the boy's confidence, of loving him and curbing his wilder instincts. A good kid at heart, but left too much on his own. 'Actually, I've always found them to be a bit of a mystery,' Des mused.

'All of them?'

'Oh, I don't mean little girls like the one who lives next door.' Des gave the boy a conspiratorial smile. Bradley and Lucy Robinson were getting along together like a house on fire. 'I was thinking more about love, relationships – things like that.'

Bradley was eyeing him shrewdly. Sometimes, to Des, he seemed older than his years. 'Did you ever fall in love?'

Hopelessly – and now it was too late. A mix-up, a misunderstanding; it hadn't been Daphne's fault. 'Yes,' he said quietly. 'Yes, I did.'

'Did you get married?' Bradley was still watching him keenly.

'Almost.' Waiting at the church, no sign of Daphne – and he had believed his run of bad luck was still dogging him, that once again there had been a last-minute change of mind. 'It didn't work out.' He smiled sadly. 'You see, Bradley, it's often not anyone's fault. It's just that...

people . . . two people . . . can't work out things together. I mean, sometimes, you try as hard as you can, but it just doesn't seem to work out.'

Later, when Bradley was asleep, Des and Andrea stood beside the bed, looking down at him. 'He looks just like you when he's asleep,' Andrea observed.

Des thought so, too. Ever since Andrea had dropped her bombshell – had presented him with this living testimonial to a warm and sweetly scented night beside the river in Perth eleven years earlier, when Des was seventeen and Andrea sixteen and they both thought they were wildly in love – he had been noting the resemblances. All the same, he felt a little sheepish. 'Yes . . . I guess so,' he murmured as a soft whimper came from the bed where the boy was beginning to stir restlessly.

'Oh, blast,' Andrea said.

'What is it?'

As he turned in the bed Bradley's fist punched down into the pillow. 'Daddy,' he moaned. 'Oh . . . Dad . . .'

Des stared at the boy. 'Did he say . . . Dad . . . Daddy?'

'He's having his nightmares again.' Bending over her son, Andrea began to stroke his face gently. 'Bradley, darling,' she whispered soothingly. 'It's all right. Mummy's here.'

Beneath her ministrations, the boy gradually relaxed. 'Does this happen often?' Des asked as Andrea straightened.

She shook her head. 'Not for a long time,' she said sombrely. 'It's just that this family business . . . this uncertainty . . . it's been such a worry.'

Once again, Des saw that his responsibilities towards the boy he was by now convinced was his son, were very real.

The following morning, Eileen Clarke found Des having his break in Daphne's coffee shop. When he saw her coming, he groaned inwardly and hid himself behind the newspaper he was reading. But it was too late, for she had already seen him.

'I've got nothing more to say, Mum,' he said as she bore relentlessly down on him.

She sat down at the table opposite him. 'Yes, there is, Desmond.' She leaned forward confidently. 'All I want is a few minutes of your time.' Feeling himself nicely trapped, Des sighed and folded his newspaper. 'I know that I have been overly protective,' she said, 'and I know that things have to change. But I want you to know that I do admire you, Desmond, for taking the stand you have with regard to that little boy. And his mother, too, of course,' she added with an obvious effort. 'I wanted you to know that before I go away.'

'You're going away?' This was news to Des.

Eileen smiled – a little smugly, Des thought. 'Well, yes,' she said. 'You know how I've been promising myself a trip for some time now. Well, now seems to be an appropriate time. I thought I would visit some old friends in Perth.'

If this was good news to Des, Andrea seemed oddly hesitant when he told her. 'Why Perth?' she demanded with a frown.

'Why not?' Des countered. 'She's got friends there. She's been promising herself this trip for quite a while.'

Andrea turned away. For the rest of that evening, she seemed quite thoughtful.

If Des had made up his mind as far as the boy was

concerned, he was still undecided about Andrea. She continued to drop hints that were none too subtle. 'Why do I have the feeling you want to talk about marriage again?' he asked.

'Des, even your mother thinks we should get married.'

'I don't want to talk about it, Andrea.'

'What about Bradley? He deserves that much.'

'I said I don't want to talk about it.'

But it still had to be faced: he did owe an enormous debt to Bradley. 'He told me he had one of his nightmares last night,' Andrea said some time later.

Des showed his disappointment. 'Why didn't he tell *me* about it?'

'Would you have been interested?'

Des was stung. 'That's not fair.'

'I'm not talking about fairness.' Andrea regarded him steadily. They were alone in the house: it was the Easter weekend and Bradley had gone on a picnic. 'I'm talking about my *son* – and where *he's* concerned anything is fair.' Her voice softened. 'Des, he does need the security of a father.'

'Well, I'm trying,' Des muttered uncomfortably.

'And until we get married,' Andrea went on, 'he will *never* regard you as a father – not in the proper sense.'

But Des didn't love her. 'I'm sorry, Andrea. I can't make that commitment.'

Andrea rose quickly to her feet. 'Then I'll just have to find someone who can,' she said crisply.

Des stared up at her in astonishment. 'What did you say?'

Her expression was taut. 'I owe it to Bradley,' she said. 'Either you marry me and accept Bradley as your legal son or I walk out of here and you'll never see him again.'

It was an ultimatum that had to be taken very seriously. Des felt worse now than ever. He decided to discuss his problem with Helen Daniels next door. Helen always had her head set squarely on her shoulders – she would think of something.

Helen made him a cup of tea. He drank it, then another. On his fourth cup she reminded him that he had come to discuss something important with her. 'Oh . . . Yes, I'm sorry, Helen,' he said awkwardly. 'I've been wasting your time.'

'It isn't that,' she said with a smile. 'It's just that I don't think I can keep drinking tea.'

It was time to take the plunge. Des took it. 'You see . . . Bradley's my son.'

Helen's smile didn't falter; there was not even a flicker to show that the revelation had come as a surprise to her. At first, Des thought she hadn't heard him.

'I said . . . Bradley's my son.'

'Yes, I heard you,' Helen returned calmly.

Des looked across the table at her in surprise. 'You knew?'

'Not really.' She shook her head slightly. 'Somewhere along the line it just crossed my mind, that's all.'

They were sitting in the kitchen of the Robinson house. There Helen quietly and efficiently coped with the needs and problems of all her grandchildren, and the son-in-law who had never married again after the death of his wife. 'Andrea wants me to marry her,' Des told her.

'Do you want to marry *her*?'

'It doesn't really matter what *I* want,' Des replied unhappily. 'What's more important is that Bradley would be my legitimate son and have a secure home.'

'Do you love her?' Helen asked quietly.

'I have responsibilities.'

'I asked you if you love her.' Then, when Des glumly shook his head, she said, 'Daphne?'

'Yes,' Des whispered. He was feeling thoroughly miserable.

'Yes what?'

'Yes. I still love Daphne.'

'Then if you still love Daphne,' Helen said with gentle emphasis, 'you shouldn't marry Andrea. It's as simple as that. By not being definite about it, you're being cruel not only to her but to yourself.'

'But what do I tell her?'

Helen thought about this for a moment, then said, 'You'll think of something. When you've made up your mind you'll find the right things to say.'

It wouldn't be easy to confront Andrea with the truth, to make her see why he couldn't marry her, but it had to be done.

'What do you mean – can't marry me?' Andrea demanded.

'It's what I said. I'm sorry.'

He had gone back to his own house, and come straight out with it – he couldn't marry her. 'I have a *son,*' she cried, pointing an accusing finger at him. '*Your* son.'

Helen had told him that the right words would come. He battled on in the face of Andrea's anger. 'It would be a loveless marriage,' he pointed out to her. 'And how long do you think *that* would last?'

'What are you talking about?' Andrea retorted. 'Passion? Romance?' She shook her head. 'How long does that last in *any* marriage?'

'Look, Andrea, that's not . . .'

'But mutual respect – that's something different. A marriage based on mutual respect can always work.'

'Do you think we're capable of respecting each other?' Des shook his own head. 'I doubt it.'

'But for Bradley's sake. He *needs* a home. Don't you care about him at *all*?'

'Of course I do.'

'Then that's all the reason you need.'

Far from it, Des thought. He was beginning to feel on surer ground now. 'I would be creating a home just like the one in which *I* was brought up,' he said fervently. 'Respect? Oh yes, respect. But loveless and cold – and in the end I would walk out on you just as my own father did.'

Andrea moved closer to him. 'It doesn't *have* to be that way, Des.' she insisted. 'I mean, you're not your father. You can make it work.'

'I would fail,' Des said flatly. 'The same as my father failed. And I wouldn't want Bradley to be eaten away by the same sadness as I was.' Even after all the years that had passed the memories were still bitter.

But Andrea was not giving up. 'We can *make* it work,' she pleaded. 'For Bradley's sake, we *must* make it work.'

'I can't.'

'Why not?'

The right words . . . The truth . . . 'Because of Daphne – that's why not.'

'Daphne?' She studied him quizzically. 'It's a little late to be thinking of Daphne, isn't it?'

'But I still love her, Andrea.' His voice quavered slightly. 'Yes, it *is* too late. But I still love her.'

'Then that's it, isn't it?' Suddenly, Andrea looked

defeated. She stared distractedly around the room. 'So that's it,' she repeated. Then she rallied. 'Well, that's it,' she said for a third time. 'I guess there's nothing else for it now but to go back to Perth. Tomorrow. Yes,' she said decisively. 'I'm taking Bradley with me.'

Des was dismayed; he hadn't expected her reaction to be so abrupt. 'That's a bit sudden, isn't it?'

Andrea looked at him bleakly. 'Well, there's no future for us here,' she said in a small voice. 'You're hardly likely to change your mind. About marriage, I mean.'

No, he hadn't changed his mind. 'Can't you stay for a while? I had planned to do things with Bradley.'

'It's too uncertain a life here,' Andrea said with a shake of her head. 'I mean, what sort of security would Bradley and I have? No, there's no point, Des. Bradley would be happier back in Perth. I've managed before, and I can manage again.'

The situation was slipping away from him again. If she went back to Perth, and took Bradley with her . . . 'Look, Andrea,' he said, thinking quickly, 'would you stay if I took on full responsibility for Bradley? It would still be as if I were his legal father. I would be responsible for all the expenses until he is old enough took after himself.'

Andrea frowned thoughtfully. 'But where would we live?'

'Here, of course,' Des replied with mounting eagerness. 'With me. You'd be free to live your own life and I'd be free to live mine. But Bradley would have both his parents here, under the one roof.' He studied her expectantly. 'What do you think?'

Her face cleared and she gave him a smile that was perfectly captivating. 'That sounds fine by me,' she said cheerfully.

They soon settled into a routine. Andrea looked after the house and made plans for renovation, beginning with new curtains. She prepared interesting meals culled from recipe books, and made no further mention of marriage. In the meantime, Des spent all his free time with Bradley, taking him out to places, organising games and other activities. One day they went to the speedway.

'Sometimes I can't help wondering how things might have turned out,' Andrea said that same evening after an exhausted Bradley had been packed off to bed.

'What? With you and me?'

'Yes. In Perth. If your mother hadn't said her piece.'

'Oh, great guns, I think,' Des said with a wry smile. 'I would have proposed, you might have accepted – and then we would have been struck down by some sort of natural catastrophe. Perhaps an earthquake.' Something, anyway– he had an abysmal record as far as marriage proposals went. Four times he had been left hovering on the brink of matrimony.

'Any girl would be lucky to marry you,' Andrea observed.

'It's a pity no one told Daphne that,' Des said drily.

'It's her loss.'

When Paul Robinson asked her out for dinner about a week later, Andrea bought a new dress.

'How do I look?'

She looked radiant. She sparkled and shimmered. Staring at her, Des experienced a small pang that was totally unexpected. He remembered a moonlit night many years before, and a girl who had been waiting for him near the river. 'You don't have to go overboard,' he said. 'It's only dinner, after all.'

She gave him a brilliant smile. 'I'll take my chances.'

'Well, I guess you know what you're doing.'

She must have picked up the slightest edge in his tone. 'We did agree, didn't we?'

'Yes, we did.' They had no claims on each other – that was the arrangement. Des would stay home with Bradley, and perhaps they would kick the football around for a while in the back yard before it became too dark. After that they would work together on the construction of the model racing-car Des had brought home for the boy.

They worked on the model in companionable silence. Des suggested they might go to the motor show the following week, and the boy had become quite excited at the prospect. 'Yes, and a couple of more years down the track,' Des said, 'I might even teach you to drive.' He would look forward to that.

'Formula One?'

'Not Formula One.'

'Drag racing then,' Bradley suggested brightly.

It was obvious that the kid liked cars. 'No. Just one step at a time, eh?'

The model was almost finished; there were just a few more of the finer details that needed to be glued together. The front door opened and Lucy Robinson walked into the room. 'Can I come in?'

'You already are.' Des smiled up at her. 'How are tricks, Lucy?'

The little girl shrugged. 'Nobody's home except Scott, and he's doing his homework. Boring. Hi, Bradley.'

'We're busy,' Bradley muttered.

Not put out by the ungraciousness of his tone, Lucy moved across to the table on which they were working.

'Can I help?'

Bradley continued to frown over the model. 'It's not for girls.'

'Well, I always help Paul with his model aeroplanes.' Lucy sat down next to him.

'She could put the tyres on the wheels,' Des suggested.

Bradley was still plainly reluctant. 'All right then. Just the tyres on the wheels.'

Des handed the wheels and the tyres to Lucy. 'When do you expect it to be finished?' she asked.

'Don't know,' Des replied. 'Maybe the day after tomorrow.'

Lucy began to fit the first tyre. 'I'll be at school for the Mother and Daughter talk,' she informed them.

'You haven't got a mother,' Bradley reminded her.

'My grandmother's taking me,' Lucy said defensively.

Seeing that there was an argument brewing between the two of them, Des tried to head it off. 'Well, Bradley's going to the next night,' he said.

Lucy's smile was small but triumphant. 'He hasn't got a father.'

'Yes, I have,' Bradley retorted.

'Not here, anyway.'

'Yes, he has.' Des placed his arm around Bradley's thin shoulders. There was no reason now why people shouldn't know. 'He's got me.'

'You mean . . .?' Lucy's eyes widened as the realisation of what she had just been told sank in. She stared at Des, then at Bradley. 'But you're . . . Are you really?'

Des nodded. 'Yes, that's right. I'm Bradley's father.'

Lucy jumped up from the chair. 'Hey, that's great,' she cried. She swung accusingly on Bradley. 'You didn't tell me.' Then, darting around the table, she hurried to the door. 'I'll be right back.'

As the door slammed behind the girl, Des was struck by a sudden doubt. Within the shortest space of time the whole street would know that he was Bradley's father. Perhaps, by making his proud announcement, he had well and truly opened a can of beans. He smiled apologetically at Bradley who was once more concentrating on his model car. 'Well, *I* don't mind people knowing,' he said. 'Do you?'

Bradley looked up at him and slowly shook his head.

'Great.' Des leaned forward in his chair to peer at the model car. 'Let's finish this then, shall we?'

Des had expected that Andrea would be pleased at what he had done - after all, it was an open acknowledgment of his relationship with the boy. There couldn't be anything wrong with that. But Andrea seemed to think there was everything wrong with it. 'I don't want my son to be the subject of every loose tongue in Ramsay Street,' she snapped.

Des thought she was over-reacting. 'A seven-day wonder, that's all,' he said. 'They'll accept it. Anyway, it's better for you - and for Bradley.'

Andrea sighed in exasperation. 'I still think you should have spoken to me about it first.'

'But I thought you *wanted* to belong,' Des said with a puzzled frown. 'I thought you *wanted* people to accept you.'

'What's Eileen going to say?' Andrea demanded.

Eileen? What did his mother have to do with it? 'What difference does that make?'

'I'm sorry,' Andrea said wearily. 'It's just that I'm tired, that's all. I have a headache.' She headed toward the hall. 'I'm going to bed.'

Still puzzled by the reference she had made to his mother, Des stared thoughtfully after her.

The following day, the subject of his speculation arrived back from Perth, having apparently cut her visit short. There was a slight breathlessness in her voice when she telephoned Des at the bank, dragging him out of a meeting, to tell him that she was back and that she had some interesting news for him. It was important that she see him immediately.

'Look, Mum, I can't come home now,' he protested. 'I'm in the middle of a meeting.'

'And *I* am in the middle of saving you from making an utter fool of yourself,' she said impatiently, just before Des hung up on her.

When he arrived home that afternoon, his mother was waiting for him. So were Andrea and Bradley, both watching her warily. 'Did you have a good trip, Mum?' he asked as Eileen strode from her chair and moved to greet him. He noticed her bag on the floor beside the chair.

'Yes. It was very interesting.' Eileen kissed her son.

'So what was all this panic on the phone?'

Eileen turned to the boy. 'Bradley, perhaps you had better go out.'

Andrea was looking quite pale. 'Why?' she demanded.

'Well, I wouldn't want to embarrass him,' Eileen returned with a grim little smile.

'Bradley, do you want to stay?' Andrea asked the boy.

'Yes, please.' Bradley was regarding Des with large, sombre eyes.

There was something strange going on. Des frowned at his mother. 'Okay. What is it? What's happening?'

With a hostile glance at Andrea, Eileen turned back to her son. 'Desmond, I can't begin to understand what possessed Andrea to bring Bradley here.'

Suddenly, Bradley sprang to his feet, and rushing across to Des, flung his arms around his waist. 'He *is* my Dad,' he wailed. 'He *is*.'

Des patted the boy's head reassuringly. 'Of course I am,' he said in a soothing tone. 'Don't be upset, mate.'

Bradley still clung tightly to him. Eileen said firmly, 'No, Desmond, you are *not* his father.' Turning back to the chair in which she had been sitting, she picked her bag up from the floor beside it. She opened the bag. 'And I have the proof right here.'

Des had had enough of this; he was totally exasperated by his mother's behaviour. 'I don't care *what* you think, Mum,' he exclaimed. 'Bradley *is* my son – there's nothing more to be said about it.'

Eileen was rummaging through her bag with increasing agitation. 'That's funny,' she murmured. 'It doesn't seem to be here.'

'What doesn't?' Des felt like shaking her. 'What's funny? What doesn't seem to be there?'

Eileen was looking extremely puzzled. 'I had a copy of Bradley's birth certificate right here, in my bag.' She wheeled angrily on Andrea. 'You took it.'

Andrea stared blankly up at her. 'What on earth are you going on about?'

'I'm going on about Bradley's birth certificate,' Eileen cried. 'I had a copy right here, in my handbag, and you' – she jabbed an accusing finger towards Andrea – 'you stole it.'

Bradley had released his hold on Des, and was edging towards the door. 'I didn't even know you *had* anything like that in your bag,' Andrea said with an expression of pained innocence. 'Why should I want to touch your handbag?'

'I don't know.' Eileen was trying to think. 'Perhaps it fell out while I was paying for the taxi.'

Des was glowering at her fiercely. She had gone too far. 'Okay, Mum, that's it,' he growled. 'I just want you to apologise to Andrea and Bradley – and then get out of here.'

'Apologise?' Eileen stared at him in surprise. 'Why? I've done nothing wrong.' She nodded towards Andrea. 'This woman has tricked you. She has lied to you.' She moved towards the telephone. 'Perhaps I should call the taxi company,' she said thoughtfully. 'They might have found it by now.'

Des barred her way. Why she bothered carrying on with this pathetic charade he had no idea. There was no point; there was obviously no certificate. It had been a bluff, that was all. 'No you won't,' he said tightly.

Eileen stopped. 'You don't believe me, do you?'

'Mum, just *go*, will you.'

'The dates are wrong . . .'

'Mum . . .'

'I can always get another one, you know.'

Des was only just managing to contain himself. 'Mum, just mind your own business,' he shouted, pointing to the door. 'And get out.'

Eileen stared back at him for a long moment, then with a sorrowful shake of her head, turned and left the room. A moment later, the front door closed forcefully behind her.

She had gone, but a small doubt had been sown. 'Andrea, tell me the truth – is he my son?'

Bradley was in his room. 'How can you possibly believe the things she's been saying?' Andrea said reproachfully.

'She said she has his birth certificate.'

Andrea shook her head. 'I told you the certificate is marked "Father Unknown". I didn't put your name down because I wanted to protect you.'

Des had to accept that. He looked at her closely. 'Andrea, you're not holding anything back from me, are you?'

'Of course not.' Defiantly, she returned his stare for a moment, then looked away.

'I mean, you would tell me – wouldn't you – if there's anything I should know?'

'I've told you everything,' Andrea said quietly. 'There's nothing else.'

Of course, he couldn't have expected his mother to leave it at that – not after all the trouble she had taken of travelling to Perth and back with one main objective in mind. It was inevitable that she should telephone him at the bank the next day and insist on meeting him at Daphne's coffee shop. It was vital, she said, that she talk to him alone.

'She has you completely under her thumb,' she explained later that afternoon when they met in the coffee shop. 'That's why I had to see you away from her.'

'That rubbish.'

Eileen was leaning forward across the table. She was speaking softly but urgently. 'I spoke to Andrea's mother in Perth,' she said. 'She had no desire to discuss Andrea. Or Bradley. She hadn't the slightest interest.'

'Sometimes I wish you felt the same way about me,' Des said wrily.

'Please, Desmond.' Eileen gestured impatiently. Des sipped his coffee; Eileen hadn't touched hers. 'I also talked to some of the neighbours. They told me that before Bradley was born Andrea was very close to a young man called McKinley. Gavin McKinley. Oh, it was quite common knowledge.'

None of this was important to Des. Andrea had lived her own life, she had seen whoever she had wanted to see, and it was no big deal. Des finished his coffee. 'Is that it? Can I go now?'

'No, wait.' Eileen clutched his arm; she had more to tell him. 'So I called every McKinley in the Perth telephone book. Only one man seemed interested. He asked a lot of questions. He took my name and telephone number, but he never called back.' She stared intently into the eyes of her only son. 'I think it was him.'

'What if it was?' Des asked with a shrug. 'You've got no right to pry into people's lives like that. It's none of your business.'

'But I thought you would be *pleased*.' Eileen was clearly hurt by his lack of concern. 'I mean, now that I have proof that Andrea is out to take you for everything she can get.'

'What proof?' Des demanded.

'Bradley's birth certificate,' she told him importantly. 'It proves he was born months before she even knew you.'

Des thoughtfully disgested this piece of information. If she was right . . . But then, did it really matter? Look, Mum,' he said deliberately. 'I'm quite happy with the way things are. I don't want to know about your snooping.'

'But you have no obligation to that woman,' Eileen

persisted. 'Or to her child.'

'I told you before – that's for me to decide.' Des glared coldly at his mother. 'Now just butt out of my life. Okay, Mum?'

In a huff, and with her coffee still untouched, Eileen rose majestically to her feet. 'You see?' she called across to Daphne behind the counter as she walked briskly out of the shop. 'That's what you get for helping your children. Ingratitude.'

After she had gone, Daphne moved around from behind the counter with a cup of coffee which she placed in front of Des. 'I suppose you heard all that,' he said gloomily.

'She's told me about it already.' Daphne sat down opposite him in the chair Eileen had just vacated. 'Do you think that guy she mentioned could be Bradley's father?'

Des shrugged. 'Makes no difference either way to me.'

She raised her eyebrows. 'Why not?'

Des had given the matter considerable thought. 'Well . . . You see . . . Having that kid around made me realise how much I want a family – and I've become really attached to him.' He smiled tightly. 'And knowing how I feel about marriage, it may be the only chance I'll have – of having a kid, I mean.'

'That's up to you,' Daphne said quietly.

'Of course it would have been different if you and I had got married.'

Daphne smiled a little forlornly. 'As you say. Things might have been.'

They thought about how different things might have been for a moment, then Daphne broke the mood of quiet contemplation by saying, with a show of brightness, 'Come on, drink your coffee before it gets cold.'

What it was that caused Bradley's panic that evening, Des didn't know. The boy wouldn't tell him, but he was clearly very frightened. All Des did know was that a few minutes after he had arrived home, Bradley burst in through the front door. He stopped when he saw Andrea, then looked uncertainly at Des. He was out of breath; he looked pale. Then, without a word, he ran into his bedroom and slammed the door. Exchanging a quick, worried glance, Des and Andrea followed him. Des tried the bedroom door. It was locked. He turned to Andrea. 'What is it?' he asked. 'What happened?'

Andrea shrugged. 'I don't know.'

'He looked as though he had seen a ghost,' Des observed. That was just how the boy had appeared to him. 'If those kids are ganging up on him again . . .' He moved back along the hall to the front door. Behind him Andrea began to knock on Bradley's door. She called his name. There was nothing out on the street that could provide a clue as to the cause of Bradley's fright. Returning to Andrea, Des shook his head, then rapped sharply on the door.

'Bradley,' he called when there was no response from inside the room. 'Come on, old son, open the door and tell us what's wrong. If it's one of the neighbours, we'll sort it out.' Since he had arrived in the street with his mother, Bradley had been a continual source of exasperation to the neighbours, so there was no knowing what might have happened. Des continued to plead with him. 'Bradley, come on, be a pal. Your mother's worried about you. So am I. Just open the door so we can talk.

Nothing's going to happen. I promise you . . .'

There was the faint sound of movement behind the door, a click, the handle turned, and then, slowly, the door opened to reveal a small boy who still looked very pale and shaken. Des smiled at him reassuringly. 'So what's all the fuss about? What were you trying to do – break the sound barrier?'

Without replying, Bradley moved past them into the living room. They followed him, 'Bradley, stop this,' Andrea ordered sharply. She looked quite tense. Des gave her a warning glance; there were better ways of handling this situation.

'Come on, mate,' he said gently to the boy. 'Let's sit down.' They sat down. 'All I want to know is, what's going on? I mean, it's a little alarming when you come rushing into the house like that and lock yourself in your room – and not tell us what's happening.'

Bradley's eyes were brimming. He shook his head. 'I have to go away,' he whimpered.

'No,' Des fervently assured him. 'Of course you don't. But if you've done something . . . I know all the people around here. You might have to say you're sorry. We'll sort it out.' He looked across at Andrea. 'Won't we?'

'Of course we will.' She smiled encouragingly at the boy. 'Is it one of the neighbours, darling?'

Bradley didn't reply. 'Oh, it can't be that serious,' Des said lightly. 'Otherwise the Ramsays and Robinsons would already be banging at the front door.'

'I didn't do anything,' Bradley said with a sullen pout.

'Then what is it?' Des urged him. 'Look, Bradley,' he went on when the boy remained obstinately silent, 'no one's going to send you away from here. This is your home for as long as you want to stay.'

'Perhaps we should leave this till later,' Andrea suggested.

It seemed like a good idea. A little time, a little patience – things would calm down before long.

In the morning, as he came into the kitchen for breakfast, he sensed he had interrupted a quiet but intense conversation between Andrea and Bradley. 'I'm sick,' Bradley accounced.

He looked at him. 'What's the matter?'

'It doesn't seem to be anything serious,' Andrea told him.

'The boy didn't look as if he were ill – a little pale but nothing more than that. 'Where does it hurt?' Des asked him.

Bradley shook his head. 'I just don't feel well,' he muttered.

'He was playing outside this morning,' Andrea told Des.

After studying him for a few more moments, Des decided that the boy was well enough to go to school. 'You can't sit around here all day,' he observed, 'and school *is* important. Look, I'll drop you off on the way to work.'

'In the car?' The boy brightened perceptibly.

'Sure. In the car.'

Bradley grinned at him; he seemed hugely relieved about something. 'I'll go and get my things.'

'There you go,' Des said to Andrea with a smile. 'Problem solved. I wish the bank was so easy.'

It was a long and busy day at the bank; Des was grateful when it was finally over. As he turned into Ramsay Street, he saw that there was some sort of commotion going on outside his house. There was quite a crowd milling about: he could see the Ramsays and the Robinsons, Daphne, and his mother who was now hurrying towards him. Something out of the ordinary was happening.

Then, as he came closer, he saw Bradley, and a man who was clutching his arm and trying to drag him towards a car. Andrea had the boy's other arm and was trying to pull him back – there seemed to be some sort of tug-o-war going on. Max Ramsay, his expression one of total ferocity, was squaring up in front of the stranger.

'It's Bradley's real father,' Eileen called to Des.

With a sudden surge of alarm, Des pushed his way through the knot of people. 'What's going on here?' he demanded.

The stranger eyed him coldly. 'I'm taking the boy back.'

Bradley was in tears. Des and Andrea managed to wrestle him away from the stranger. 'No, you're not,' Andrea cried breathlessly as Des placed a protective arm around the boy.

The stranger glared at Des. 'That's my son.'

Des shook his head. 'No one's taking him anywhere,' he said with gritty determination.

Des and the man confronted each other squarely. Des realised in a flash that he must be the Gavin McKinley his mother had told him about. 'Listen, mate,' McKinley said gruffly with a jerk of his head towards Andrea. 'I don't know what she's told you, but whatever it is, it's a pack of lies. Bradley is my son, and I'm taking him back.'

Hardly aware of the small crowd that surrounded them, Des continued to stare with hostility at the rather good-looking stranger. 'That's strange,' he remarked. 'Bradley doesn't seem too pleased to see you.'

'That's because I gave him a bit of a fright, turning up out of the blue like that.' He held his hand out to the boy, 'Come on, Brad,' he said with a smile. 'Say hello to your old Dad.'

Bradley didn't take the proffered hand; he bit it instead. Gavin yelped, and made as if to strike Bradley who shrank more closely against Des's side. 'You leave him alone,' Des growled threateningly.

Gavin's tone was just as savage. 'Listen, pal, do yourself a favour and keep right out of this.'

Des made a lunge at the other man. 'You touch that kid,' he yelled, 'and I'll . . .'

Jim Robinson grabbed his arm and pulled him away. 'Hang on, Des,' he said firmly. 'No fighting.' He turned to Gavin. 'I suggest you get out of here. If you don't we'll call the police.'

'I can handle this, Jim,' Des muttered resentfully.

Apparently realising for the first time the strength of the opposition that was ranged against him, Gavin McKinley, now looking quite unsure of himself, began to back away towards his car. 'Look, I didn't come here to start a fight,' he said. 'All I want is my kid back.'

'Listen to him,' Eileen Clarke urged her son. 'It's true. He *is* Bradley's real father.'

Des looked at her, than at Gavin McKinley, who said, 'Bradley was living with me until she shot through with him.'

The seeds of doubt had been sown; Des didn't know what to think. The man *seemed* genuine enough. 'All right,' he said after a brief and thoughtful pause. 'I'll listen to what you have to say.' He nodded towards the house behind him. 'Just come inside.'

Andrea began to protest; she seemed quite agitated. 'No, Des. Please.'

'He says he's Bradley's father.' The man had a right to be heard at least.

'But, Des . . .'

'I want to hear what he has to say,' Des said, holding Bradley tight against him as he turned back to the house.

Eileen was about to follow him when Andrea rounded angrily on her. She almost screamed. 'Don't you *dare* put a foot inside this house. You've done enough damage.'

'You've fooled Desmond long enough,' Eileen flared back at her. 'This time he's going to hear the truth.'

Des stopped and swung back to face his mother. He was very annoyed. 'You keep out of this, Mum,' he said harshly. 'This is between Gavin, Andrea and me – and Bradley. So now, you just mind your own business – do you hear me? You just stay away.'

But Eileen wasn't to be put off as easily as that. Undeterred, she followed them into the house where Des, pacing up and down the length of the living room, proceeded to establish the truth of the matter.

'All right,' he said to Gavin, 'let me get this straight. Andrea gave you reason to believe that you're Bradley's father. That's why you took custody of him.'

Before Gavin had a chance to reply, Eileen said with just a hint of malicious triumph, 'There's no doubt about it, Desmond. It's exactly as I told you.'

Des turned to her. 'You've seen the birth certificate.' He pointed to Gavin, who was sitting at one end of the couch from where he had been exchanging wary glances with Andrea at the other end. 'Was his name on it?'

'Well, no . . .'

Des nodded in grim satisfaction. 'Then it could be me, couldn't it?'

Gavin glared at Andrea. 'She told me *I* was the father.'

'Did you?' Des asked Andrea.

Andrea shifted uncomfortably. 'I might have,' she murmured. 'But . . .'

Eileen interrupted again. 'It's about time you started telling the truth, young lady.'

'Why don't you just butt out?' Andrea retorted, springing to her feet and advancing threateningly on the older woman.

Eileen stood her ground. 'I'm not about to have my son made a fool of by a shameless trickster like yourself,' she returned passionately. She looked across at her son. 'Desmond, give the boy to Mister McKinley,' she said. 'He must be anxious to return to Perth.'

'This boy leaves here over my dead body,' Andrea cried, moving to the side of the armchair in which Bradley was sitting and watching these exchanges with wide, frightened eyes. Perching herself on the arm of the chair, she placed her arm protectively around his shoulders and hugged him close to her.

'Oh, it's a little late to play the hysterical mother, young lady,' Eileen went on relentlessly. 'You were only too happy to give him away the first time.'

Des's temper was on a very short fuse. 'Okay, Mum, that's it,' he said tersely. 'One more word and you're out.'

Eileen still tried to make him see reason. 'Desmond, she has fooled you. I'm only trying to see justice done. She has fooled you – can't you see that?'

'That's for me to decide.' Des glowered at her.

'She has lied to you.'

'Mum.' As Eileen faltered into silence, Des turned back to Gavin McKinley. 'Maybe we can get to the bottom of this,' he said. 'If you *do* care so much about Bradley, why didn't you take him on when he was born?'

Gavin was sitting forward on the couch. He spread his hands in a gesture of appeal. He spoke earnestly. 'Look, I admit I didn't want to know about him at first. Then my conscience got the better of me. That's why I looked up Andrea. And she couldn't wait to get him off her hands. For a price, of course. Twenty thousand dollars.'

'You offered that,' Andrea said in a strained voice. Her face was drawn, her eyes hard. 'And I really believed that Bradley would be better off with you.' Her lips tightened in a bitter smile. 'Well, that was the biggest mistake I ever made.' She looked up at Des. 'He doesn't care about Bradley. All he wants is the money. His father had threatened to cut him out of his will if he didn't produce an heir. And old McKinley is worth millions.'

Des was startled to hear this. Of course, it put the matter into an entirely different perspective. Gavin was appealing to him again. 'I just wanted to make sure the kid had a proper upbringing,' he said. 'And that's more than *she* could ever do.'

'At least I loved him,' Andrea cried in a trembling voice. 'You never have. His own father, and . . .'

She stopped abruptly; she had said too much. She had left herself open to attack – and Eileen attacked.

'Ah, you see?' There was a gleam of triumph in her eyes. 'You see? She has admitted it. I told you, Desmond. *Now* will you listen to me?'

It was the last straw. Des pointed to the door. 'Okay, Mum, that's it. Out.'

'But Desmond . . .'

Taking her roughly by the arm, he led her to the door. 'I said *out*.'

'All right.' Eileen made an obvious effort to retain her dignity. 'If you *do* insist on taking care of this yourself, I shall wait at home until such time as you care to apologise.'

'Goodbye, Mum.' Des closed the door firmly behind her, then returned to the living room.

Gavin McKinley was on his feet. 'Well, now that we've finally cleared up this misunderstanding,' he said, 'I think Bradley and I should be on our way.'

Andrea was staring pleadingly at Des. 'Des.'

His eyes glistening, Bradley was shaking his head woefully. 'I don't *want* to go back to Perth,' he whimpered.

'Don't worry, mate,' Des assured him, then turned back to Gavin. 'You haven't said anything to make me change my mind. Bradley stays.'

'But Andrea has *admitted* I'm the kid's father,' Gavin protested. His face hardened. 'If I have to take this to court, I will.'

Des called his bluff. 'Go ahead. But as your name isn't on the birth certificate, you won't have a leg to stand on.'

'I'm not giving up,' Gavin warned him. 'I've got twenty grand invested in that kid.'

'If that's what you're woried about,' Des retorted, 'then take me to court. See how far you get.'

Gavin was not looking so assured now. He glanced uncertainly at Andrea. 'Goodbye, Gavin,' she said.

He glared at Des. 'You haven't heard the last of this,' he said angrily as he made for the door.

As the door closed behind him, Des breathed a sigh of relief. It had been a tense few moments, but now it looked as if everything would be all right. He didn't expect any more trouble from that quarter. He sat down next to Bradley. 'I guess this means you're stuck with Mum and me,' Bradley remarked.

Des smiled. 'Yes, I guess it does.'

That evening, after Bradley had gone to bed, Des and Andrea had a long and serious talk. 'You've known all along, haven't you?' Andrea said. 'That Bradley is not your son.'

Not all along. There had been a time... 'I didn't realise for a while,' he told her. 'But... What with Mum coming back from Perth and making all those noises...' He thought of something. 'What did happen to that birth certificate, by the way? She was so sure she had it. Did you take it from her bag?'

'Bradley did,' Andrea replied. 'I scolded him. I told him it was very wrong. But you must understand. He was extremely upset by what was happening.'

'Yeah, well...' Des nodded thoughtfully. The kid had been having quite a hard time of it. 'Anyway, what with Mum, then Gavin showing up. I guess where there's smoke, there's fire.'

'I'm sorry,' Andrea said softly. 'I had no right to deceive you.'

'Why don't you tell the the whole story?' Des suggested.

Andrea was silent for a long moment. Then she nodded.

'Believe me,' she began in a subdued tone, 'ever since Bradley was born I've done my best. But a single mother's pension isn't much to live on, and my parents had disowned me. And it's just impossible to hold down a job when you've got a baby to look after.' She sighed. Des, watching her, saw that her recollections were painful. 'Anyway, about a year ago, things got really bad. I didn't have a job. I didn't have any money, and my landlady was threatening to evict me.'

Des could guess what happened next. 'And then Gavin turned up?'

'That's right,' Andrea said. 'He was straight with me – I'll give him that much. He didn't want me. He just wanted Bradley so that his father wouldn't cut him out of his will. I didn't really want to give Bradley up, but Gavin swore that he would have the best of everything. And with his father's money I knew that was true. So –' she smiled wanly – 'he drew up an agreement. I signed it; I had no choice. I had to promise not to go anywhere near Bradley – not to see him, or interfere in his life in any way. And for that I got twenty thousand dollars.' Her eyes were glistening; she shook her head. 'Bradley was so upset. I knew then that I couldn't stick to the agreement. I promised him that I would come back for him as soon as I had made some money.'

'What went wrong?' Des prompted when she hesitated.

'I was stupid,' she replied. 'I met a man who told me he operated a chain of boutiques in Western Australia. He asked me if I would like to invest in them. He painted a very rosy picture, told me that I could make a fortune. I believed him. I gave him the money – and didn't see him again. I was such a fool. Then, because Bradley was no longer with me, my parents took me back. Later, I heard that you were doing really well for yourself over here. It got me thinking. I remembered how well we got along together – before your mother put a spanner in the works.' Des smiled. That was true enough. 'So I borrowed some money,' Andrea went on. 'I grabbed Bradley out of boarding school, and . . . and you know the rest.'

'You must have felt very sure that you could convince me I was the father,' Des remarked.

'I knew you wouldn't throw us out,' Andrea said, 'even if you did have your doubts. You've always been too soft for your own good.'

Des thought she was probably right. He always had been a soft touch. 'Are you sure that Gavin doesn't love Bradley?' he asked.

Andrea shook her head. 'He doesn't care about Bradley at all. He just wants the money.'

'Yeah.' Des nodded slowly, then said, with determination, 'Well, he's not going to get him back. Bradley is going to stay with people who care about him.'

With a cry of joy, Andrea threw her arms around his neck. Des grinned. As Bradley had said earlier, it looked as if was stuck with them.

Two

It was all arranged. Dinner for two, soft lights and music, wit and charm, romance in the air . . . there was no telling where it could lead. Max Ramsay rubbed his hands together in gleeful anticipation. Ah yes – romance. Max was a very happy man.

He and Laura would have the house to themselves. The kids would be out, and Madge had taken him up on his offer of a ticket to the movies. Dinner, too – there had been some hard bargaining. A small snag had arisen when she flatly refused to cook the dinner for them, but then, after tackling the problem head on, he had come up with his great idea. 'I know,' he had exclaimed brightly. 'I'll ring one of those gourmet home delivery places. They only charge about sixty bucks for two and you get three courses.' It was a simple solution to the problem. A weight had been lifted from his mind.

Laura Dennison was staying with the Robinsons next door. She had come down from Queensland to visit her daughter, Nicki, who was also staying there. Max had been taken with her from the moment he first set eyes on her. She was good fun, brisk and hearty – just Max's type of woman. He was expecting her at seven-thirty.

He ordered the gourmet meal. Because he didn't have much of a clue when it came to foreign food, he left it to the restaurant to choose the dishes for him. He was prepared to be surprised.

'It will be here in half an hour,' he said as he replaced the receiver. 'How's that for service, eh?'

'Then I'll be able to eat before I go out,' Danny said, coming into the room with Max's tie rack.

'No way,' Max scowled at him. 'That gourmet tucker is for two, Laura and me – nobody else. And what are you doing with my ties?'

'I thought I might borrow some,' Danny told him. 'Wide ones are back in.'

'Really?' Madge looked up from the magazine she was reading. 'But they're antiques.'

'Oh, not the loud ones – the . . . the mod . . . the blue and greens.'

'They're my good ties,' Max protested.

'Dad, you only wear them at union meetings,' Danny reminded him. 'And funerals.'

Max conceded the point. 'All right,' he said. 'I don't suppose it will hurt to lend them.'

It was already after seven, and neither Madge nor Danny were making any great effort to move. Max glanced meaningfully at his watch. 'Well, it's quarter past seven already.'

'So subtle, Max,' Madge returned drily.

'Oh, there's no rush,' Danny said airily. 'The movie doesn't start till half past eight.'

'What are you going to see?' Madge asked him.

'I thought I might see *Eureka Stockade*,' he told her.

Madge showed interest. 'The original? With Chips Rafferty?'

'Yep, that's the one. Authority versus the rebels. Do you want to come?'

'Yeah, Madge,' Max urged his sister. 'You ought to.'

'Thank you, Danny,' Madge said with a smile. 'I'd love to come. Your father's paying. He's also kindly offered to pay for dinner.'

'Yeah, yeah.' Max gestured impatiently.

'Well, are you ready for your little tête-à-tête?' Madge asked him.

'Now don't jump the gate,' Max said shortly. 'It's only dinner, a bit of a chat – that's all.'

'And that's all I meant,' Madge returned. 'But if you *do* feel romance tugging at your heart, don't get heavy. Women like the gentle approach.'

She was getting at him again. 'Do you mind?' Max growled. 'Anyway . . .' he glanced at his watch again, 'it's about time you two got a wriggle on, isn't it? You don't want to miss the start of the film.'

Danny picked out one of his father's ties from the rack and held it up. It was a bright irridescent blue and green and had a picture of a naked woman on it; it had been one of Max's favourites. 'Where did this come from?'

'Never you mind.' Grabbing the tie from Danny's hand, Max shoved it quickly into his pocket.

Danny shrugged. 'Beggars can't be choosers, I guess,' he said, then to Madge, 'I'll be about twenty minutes.'

Max was finding it hard to keep his patience. He glanced at his watch again. Laura would be arriving any minute now. He sighed.

They were still there when the food arrived in silver bowls. Madge and Danny made a great show of lifting the lids and sniffing the contents. They looked mightily impressed.

'What's this?' Danny asked. 'Baby food?'

Madge critically examined the bowl in question. 'It looks like vichyssoise.'

'No, I think it's leek soup.' Danny looked up at his father who had just had a quick wash and a change of clothes and was looking particularly smart. 'Dad, all this looks a bit weird. What did you order?'

'I didn't order,' Max told him. 'They had a choice – five complete meals, see, and I got number five.'

'The cheapest, naturally,' Madge remarked.

'Wrong as usual,' Max said a little smugly. 'Damn near the most expensive.' Hang the expense, he had told himself; let money be no object. He was out to make an impression.

Madge looked unimpressed. 'Well, I'm glad it's not for me,' she said. 'If I'm eating a meal I like to know what it is.'

Max felt suddenly disconcerted. She was right, of course. At the table, which had already been set, Danny was still peering into the bowls. 'Dad, this one here, at the end – looks like snails.'

'Eh?' Max moved to his son's side and looked down into the bowl. Danny was pulling his leg. It didn't look like snails; it looked like . . . 'Don't be ridiculous.' He replaced the lid quickly.

'It's gourmet food, Max,' Madge reminded him. 'If it's not snails, it's frogs' legs or some other foreign delicacy.'

Max had had enough of this. 'All right,' he growled. 'You've had your little joke. Now how about getting a move on? You don't want to miss the main film.'

'Oh, there's no rush,' Danny said teasingly. 'They only have those boring ads.'

'Then perhaps you could fill your aunt with choc tops until the main feature,' Max suggested tersely. 'Because you're not staying here.'

There was a knock at the door. Max was suddenly nervous. His date had arrived. 'That'll be Laura,' Madge said, moving out into the hall. 'I'll get it.'

Before Max could stop her, she had opened the door, brightly greeted Laura, and was now ushering her into the room. 'Max is as ready for you as he'll ever be,' she was saying. 'I'm going out tonight. Danny is escorting me to a movie.'

Laura was wearing a dark green dress; she had done something with her hair. She smiled warmly at Max. 'Yeah, g'day, Laura,' Max said awkwardly, then, moving across to Madge and Danny who were still hovering around, began to push them out of the room. 'Enjoy your movie,' he said.

Finally, they were out of the house. 'Cleared the decks, have you?' Laura asked as he rejoined her.

'That's right.' Max beamed at her. 'At least we've got the place to ourselves. So now . . .' He rubbed his hands together . . . 'What will you have? Beer? Or maybe a sherry?'

'Oh, I'd kill for a beer.'

Yes, she was definitely his kind of woman. 'You're on,' he said approvingly, placing an arm around her shoulders and leading her into the kitchen. 'Let's go and raid the fridge.'

Max had obviously gone to a lot of trouble. Later, as he was wrestling with a bottle of champagne, Laura commented on the fact. 'Did you buy the champagne especially for me?' she asked.

They were seated at the table. The silver bowls were

arranged between them. Max had also put out a couple of candles for effect. 'Yeah, nothing but the best. Oh . . .'

Suddenly, with a very loud retort, the cork flew straight up out of the bottle with stunning force and shattered the light bulb above their heads. Laura screamed. The room was plunged into darkness. A foamy stream cascaded from the bottle. Max placed his thumb over it. 'Oh,' he said.

Now Laura was laughing. 'Hey, what happened?'

He tried to make her out in the darkness. This wasn't a good start to the proceedings at all. 'Must have busted the light bulb,' he observed. Placing the bottle on the table, he stood up. 'Just stay there. I'll get another one.'

'No, it's okay,' Laura said. 'I've got some matches in my bag.'

'Eh?'

A match flared and scattered shadows across Laura's face as, leaning forward, she directed the flame to the wick of one of the candles. A moment and two more matches later, both candles were alight. Laura looked very dim and alluring in the flickering candlelight. Max chuckled. 'Hey, that's great. You know, I was going to suggest we turn down the lights anyway.'

Laura nodded. 'Yes, it's much more romantic.'

'And not only that,' Max said with some relief. 'It might be as well if we don't see the food too clear.'

'Why's that?'

Max was beginning to feel a little shy. 'Promise you won't laugh?'

'Mmmmm.'

'I really don't know what we're eating,' he confessed.

Laura laughed. 'How come?'

'Well, I was going to pretend I cooked it all, see, but

I... I knew you would catch on.' He laughed self-deprecatingly. 'It's gourmet takeaway – and I don't know what it is.'

Laura was treating it as a huge joke. 'Oh, Max, you're a gem,' she exclaimed. 'You went to all this trouble because of me?'

'Well... it's not exactly how I planned it.'

'Oh, Max,' Laura said with great affection. 'You're a real nice bloke.'

'Ah...'

She raised the lid from one of the bowls. 'I don't know what you've got here but it smells terrific.'

By now Max was brimming over with goodwill. 'You're a good sort, Laura.'

Laura replaced the lid. 'Oh...'

'I mean it,' Max said fervently. 'You're just yourself – you know what I mean?'

'That's all I've ever been,' she said with a sigh. 'But it's not good enough for some people.'

'It's good enough for me.' When he saw that she had picked up the ladle to begin dishing out the food, Max said, 'Hang on there. Let's not eat yet. We haven't toasted ourselves.' He filled the two glasses from the champagne bottle and passed one of them across to her. 'Here you go.'

Smiling at each other across the pool of candlelight, they gently touched their glasses. 'To you,' Max said softly.

Laura shook her head. 'To us.'

They touched their glasses again. They sipped their champagne.

The food was excellent. Afterwards they sat together on the living room sofa with their coffee and cheese on the low table in front of them. The candles, which they brought with them from the dinner table, still cast a gentle glow over the room. Max had put on some music; a hundred strings soared and swooped gently in the background. It was a perfect setting for Laura and Max as they discussed the last football Grand Final.

'I haven't missed one in six years,' Laura said.

'Well, I'll be blowed.' Max shook his head in bemusement, then placed his hand over Laura's. 'Let's go together next time.'

'Okay. It's a date.'

Max smiled at her. 'You know all about sport, don't you? I mean, you talk about it as if you were a bloke.'

Laura laughed. 'Oh, Max . . .'

'Mmmm?'

'If I were a bloke would we be sitting on the couch here by candlelight?'

She had a point. 'No, I suppose not.' He expanded on this. 'If you was a bloke I wouldn't be holding your hand.'

They chuckled at the idea. Raising Max's arm, Laura placed it around her shoulder. 'Or put your arm around me,' she said.

Her face was so close to his; there was an inviting gleam in her eyes; her lips were moist and slightly parted; Max's heart began to perform a little patter.

He was poised, he was just on the verge, drawing even closer, their lips just on the point of meeting – when the front door opened. He heard Madge's voice, then Danny's. Startled, he jumped away from Laura to the other end of the sofa. He tried to look nonchalant.

'They were the country's first entrepreneurs,' Danny was saying.

'They were breaking the law,' Madge said. They were discussing the movie. Suddenly, the room was full of harsh and unrelenting light. Max blinked. 'There, that's better,' said Madge.

'You missed a great movie, Dad,' Danny said cheerfully.

Max glared at his relatives who had just succeeded in ruining his night for him. 'Oh, yeah...'

'Chips Rafferty was *wonderful*,' Madge said. 'He played Peter Lalor, the leader of the rebels.'

'They weren't rebels,' Danny sat down in one of the armchairs. 'They were reformists.'

'Danny.' Madge gave him a reproachful look.

'Well, when they refused to pay their licence fees they were aiming a punch at Big Government.'

Irritated as he was by the interruption, Max found himself being drawn into the argument despite himself. 'The Government?' he exclaimed testily. 'That bunch of no-hoper gold miners? They wouldn't even *know* what Big Government was. They were just fighting for themselves – fighting for the common man.'

'Peter Lalor did all right out of it, though,' Danny observed. 'He used the revolt to get himself into politics. Clever move. Free publicity. Media did it all for him.'

'Yeah... I reckon the television should stay out of politics.' Max opined. 'I mean, nine of out of ten voters these days vote for the politician who comes across best on the box.'

Danny was looking at him strangely. 'Dad, the Eureka Stockade was more than a hundred years ago. The gold rush – remember?'

'Come on, Danny,' Madge was edging towards the kitchen. She gave him a meaningful look.

'Oh, yeah...' Danny was on his feet. He glanced at Laura. 'Sorry, Dad.'

'Would you like me to turn the light off again?' Madge asked.

'Do me a favour,' Max said grimly. What did it matter? The mood was shattered, anyway, candlelight or not.

Madge switched off the light. 'Just carry on as if we weren't here,' she said pleasantly. 'Danny, would you like a cup of tea?'

Laura and Max sat side by side in the muted glow from the candles. Max looked helplessly at Laura. Laura smiled back at him. Danny's head popped around the corner of the door. 'Hey, Dad, what's up with the light in the kitchen?' he queried.

Laura thought that was very funny; she began to laugh.

Of course, there was nothing else for it but to give in to Madge's insistence that he change the light bulb. He might as well – Laura had already gone, and in the other room the surging strings had taken on a decidedly gypsy flavour. 'I still can't see why it couldn't have waited until morning,' he muttered after he had changed the bulb with unconcealed ill grace and stepped down from the table.

Madge had made tea for herself and Danny. 'Because tomorrow would have never come,' she said.

There was no hope now; the evening was in tatters. Romance had gone out the door with Laura, who had thanked him for the lovely dinner, for the very nice time she'd had, but it *was* getting rather late...

'Oh, you showed heaps of class tonight, Dad,' Danny said, helping himself to some cheese. 'Great food.'

'Hey, you get your grubby maulers off that,' Max yelped. He glowered at them both. 'Now I'd just like to say thank you very much for wrecking the only decent evening I've had in years.'

'But you heard Laura,' Madge protested. 'She said the evening was fine.'

'It wasn't over yet.'

'Oh, I see . . .' Madge's tone was heavily larded with meaning.

Max could feel the sudden warmth in his cheeks. 'And don't get the wrong idea,' he said quickly. 'All I meant was . . .' He faltered. 'All I meant . . .'

'Sorry, Dad,' Danny said with a mischievous glint in his eye. 'You should have warned us.'

'Now don't get smart.'

'Then you should put a sign in the window,' Danny suggested lightly. 'Or something.'

Max silenced him with a look. 'Look, all I wanted . . . I mean, all I wanted was a little privacy, a chance for some intelligent conversation with a lady I respect, in my own flamin' house, for pete's sake.'

'Now hang on there,' Madge said crisply. 'The house is only half yours, so don't start all that up again. And as for intelligent conversation with a lady you respect . . .' She smiled grimly and shook her head. 'It's your sister you're talking to, you know. I wasn't born yesterday. You didn't lay out a fortune on gourmet food just to finish off the evening with a game of Trivial Pursuit.'

Max began to protest. 'Ah . . . now hang on . . .'

But with an expression of supreme disapproval, Madge overrode him. 'How your two boys have survived your dreadful example, I just do not know.' With a nod to Danny, she turned on her heel. 'I'm going to bed now.

Goodnight.'

'Me, too,' Danny said. He winked at his father. 'Goodnight, Dad.'

'Struth,' Max exclaimed after they had gone to their rooms. 'A man just can't win.' He felt utterly defeated.

Three

If it hadn't been for Clive Gibbons, Lucy Robinson would almost certainly have died as a result of a bee sting.

When she had come into the kitchen gasping for breath they had thought at first that she was playing one of her silly little games. It was her grandmother who was the first to realise that she wasn't. By that time the girl was gradually slipping into unconsciousness. Helen Daniels had ordered Scott to run next door to fetch Clive. They could only hope and pray that he was there. Thankfully, as it turned out, he was.

It had been a long time since Clive had given up medicine, preferring a much more undisciplined and less secure – and therefore, he said, an infinitely more interesting – existence. But faced with an emergency, as this undoubtedly was, the old training came quickly to the fore.

Scott had already called an ambulance, but Clive didn't think they could afford to wait for it to arrive. Something had to be done – and fast: the girl was struggling for breath, she was turning blue. 'We'll have to do a tracheotomy,' Clive decided. 'Scott, help me get her up on to the table.'

Gently, they lifted her up. Clive turned to Helen. 'I'll need some methylated spirits, and cotton wool. And Scott, get me a biro and the sharpest knife.'

Clive saw the angry red spot on the girl's neck and recognised it as a bee sting. He took the pen from Scott and broke it in half. 'Okay, give me the knife,' he ordered after he had cleaned the wound with cotton wool soaked in methylated spirits. 'I have to make an incision in her throat so she can breathe,' he explained to Helen who was watching him with a concerned expression. 'The bee sting has caused her air passage to contract.'

He worked quietly, and efficiently. After the area had been thoroughly cleansed he inserted the empty pen case into the incision he had made so that the girl could breathe. Her breathing was still irregular, but until the ambulance arrived, she would be safe.

By the time Paul Robinson came home that evening, Helen and Scott had returned from the hospital after being assured that Lucy was out of danger, although she would have to remain there under observation for a while. Lucy was a very lucky girl, they had been told. The tracheotomy had almost certainly saved her life.

'What's been going on here?' Paul asked when he saw the mess on the kitchen table.

Scott told him what had happened. Paul was shocked. 'Clive had to operate right here,' his brother said. 'On the table.'

'It's something I wouldn't want to live through again,' Helen said faintly; she looked quite drawn.

'Where's Dad?' Paul asked. 'Is he still at the hospital?'

Now Helen was looking quite troubled. 'We haven't seen your father all day,' she replied. 'Or heard from him. He just hasn't been home.'

It was already after nine thirty. 'He should be home,' Paul said in surprise. 'I left them over three hours ago. They should be back by now.' The more he thought about it, the more appalled he became.

'They?' His grandmother was watching him closely. 'Who was he with?'

'Zoe,' Paul replied unhappily. 'I left him and Zoe together.'

And this was the problem; Zoe and his father were seeing far too much of each other; Paul didn't like the way things seemed to be developing between them. For one thing – the main thing, really – Zoe was young enough to be Jim Robinson's daughter. She was also Paul's secretary. It wasn't right; it wasn't healthy.

There had been some papers that had urgently needed signing and notarising, then despatched to Rosemary Daniels in New York that same evening. Paul had been out of town, inspecting some property in which, as Rosemary's representative, he thought the corporation would be interested. He had been startled when Zoe had turned up at the property with his father, who had driven her there, with the papers for him to sign. Paul had driven straight back to the city with the papers.

I suppose they *did* say they were coming straight back?' Helen said thoughtfully when Paul had explained this to her.

'Well, no,' Paul said hesitantly. 'But I just naturally assumed...'

'They could have had an accident,' Scott suggested.

'We would have heard if they had,' Helen said.

'Well, then, they might have stopped off for a meal or something.' Scott looked shrewdly at his older brother. 'I don't know what you're getting so uptight about,

Paul.'

Paul thought there was plenty to get uptight about; he was very angry with his father. Striding across to the refrigerator, he took out a can of beer for himself. 'What do you expect, Scott?' he demanded bitterly. 'While our sister is desperately ill in hospital, her father's off in the bush chasing a bit of fluff.'

'Paul!' Helen looked shocked. 'Don't talk about your father like that.'

Scott was also looking at him reproachfully, Paul didn't care *what* they thought. 'I know Zoe,' he returned defiantly. 'She's a piranha.'

'You're off your head,' Scott said sharply.

'She's my secretary, mate,' Paul reminded him tersely. 'Maybe I'd know her a little better than you would.'

The telephone rang.

Before it could develop into a real fight, the telephone rang. Helen answered it. 'Jim,' she exclaimed in mingled annoyance and relief. 'Where on earth have you been? I've been worried sick.' Paul and Scott listened to her end of the conversation. 'Well, I'm very pleased for you, I'm sure,' she said after listening to her son-in-law for a moment. 'However, if it isn't too much trouble, I suggest you get here immediately... Yes, there *is* something. Lucy's ill. She's in hospital. She has been asking for you... No, no, she's in good care. There's nothing to be alarmed about... Yes, but get here.' She replaced the receiver and turned back to her two grandsons. 'Apparently, he's staying in a motel with a very beautiful and charming lady,' she said flatly. 'That's what he told me, anyway.'

Paul was furious. 'Hang on there,' he cried. 'Just let

me get this straight. You mean, while my sister is lying there in hospital, he's been...'

Helen's voice cut across his. 'Don't over-react, Paul.'

'Over-react?' Paul flared at her. 'How am I *supposed* to react?' He stormed away to his room.

He was lying awake when his father arrived home about two hours later. He was still fuming. As he heard the front door open, then the sound of movement in the hall, he leapt out of bed and hurriedly donned his dressing gown.

The living room light was on. Paul confronted his father, who was looking strained and anxious. 'I was wondering when you were going to show up,' he said coldly.

'How is she?' Jim asked quietly. 'Is there any change?'

'She's all right.'

Jim glanced at his watch. 'I suppose it's too late for me to go over there now.'

'And it was also too late a few hours ago when she needed you,' Paul said acidly, 'It's such a pity that you were tied up... elsewhere.'

A flicker of annoyance passed across Jim's face. 'The car broke down.' He tossed his keys on to the table. 'These things happen.'

Paul didn't believe him. 'Oh, come on, Dad, that's an old line. I would have thought you could have come up with something better than that.'

'There was nothing in it, Paul,' Jim said wearily. 'I just didn't see the point in coming all the way back to town, then going out again in the morning to pick up the car.'

'It was easy enough when you needed to.'

'We got a lift,' Jim muttered.

Paul laughed mirthlessly. 'Oh, how convenient.'

There was a warning note in Jim's voice. 'We had separate rooms, Paul.'

'Oh, sure.'

Jim regarded his son bleakly. 'I'm tired,' he said, 'and I don't feel I have to justify my actions to you. And quite frankly, right now I don't give a damn whether you believe me or not.'

Paul followed him out of the living room. 'Well, just for the record, I don't.'

Jim shrugged heavily. 'Fine.'

Paul couldn't resist another jab. 'And also for the record, I happen to think this whole thing is pretty damn sordid.'

Jim rounded on him angrily. 'Paul . . .' He hesitated. 'I'll talk to you about this in the morning when we're both more rational.'

'I happen to feel perfectly rational right now,' Paul said flatly. 'I also have a rational interest in my family. It's a pity you don't feel the same way . . . Dad.'

Back in his room, Paul still couldn't sleep; his thoughts churned furiously. His father and Zoe Davis . . . He still couldn't believe it was happening. It was an impossible situation. Zoe was still only a kid – it was too ridiculous. Even then, as he thought about them, his father and Zoe, Paul couldn't admit to himself that he might have been jealous.

He was already in the office the following morning when Zoe arrived. 'Oh hello,' she said when she saw him behind his desk. 'I thought you were out of the office all morning.'

'I changed a few appointments,' he said distantly.

'Oh, I see.' She placed her bag down on her desk. Paul sensed that she was trying to appear more casual than she actually was; there seemed to be a certain self-consciousness about her movements. 'For any particular reason?'

Paul eyed her sternly. 'Zoe, you can drop the act. You're not fooling anybody – except maybe yourself.'

Zoe moved around behind her own desk, sat down and removed the cover from her typewriter. She didn't look at him. 'Paul, what *are* you on about?'

Rising to his feet, Paul moved across to her desk. 'I want this business between my father and you to stop – right now,' he said, leaning over her.

'Oh yes, sir,' she returned sarcastically. 'Right away, sir.' A muscle twitched at the corner of her mouth.

Paul frowned down at her. 'Hey, we're not talking about some guy you just picked up in a bar.'

'I don't pick up men in bars, thank you very much.' Zoe's voice was brittle. She looked up at him with a puzzled expression. 'Paul, what are you getting so upset about?' she asked.

'Just how far has the thing gone?' he demanded.

'It's gone nowhere.' Pushing her chair back, Zoe stood up and moved around the desk to face Paul. 'Look, Paul, your father is a very attractive man, and given the opportunity I'd like to get to know him a lot better.' She looked at him steadily for a long moment. 'Now can I get on with my work?'

Paul could feel the bitterness rising up inside him. Roughly, he grabbed her arm; his fingers dug into her flesh. Zoe gasped; he knew he was hurting her.

'Let go of me!'

'But if it's a man you want . . .' Before she could react, he pulled her to him, holding her tightly with both arms as his lips crushed brutally down on hers. There was no response; Zoe's body remained rigid. After a moment, Paul released her.

'Thanks,' Zoe said, very coldly, 'but no thanks. You're not really my type.'

Paul didn't know what he had really expected; perhaps he really had expected her to respond. But she had rejected him, and now he felt foolish – angry, too, but mainly with himself. He glared at her, then moved back to his own desk.

Relations between them remained strained for most of the day. They worked for the most part in an oppressive silence; Paul was still smouldering from his rebuff; Zoe was very cool. She answered the telephone when it rang, and switched the calls through if they were for Paul. She made notes and with calm efficiency typed the letters Paul had dictated to her; she filed and sorted and made appointments for Paul.

About halfway through the afternoon Rosemary Daniels called from New York, to advise Paul she had received the papers he had despatched the previous evening. 'Rosemary's pleased,' he said as he put down the receiver.

'I'm sure,' Zoe said drily. 'You didn't give *me* any credit, I noticed.'

'Now hang on . . .'

'If I hadn't chased you,' Zoe interrupted his protest, 'Rosemary wouldn't have had her precious papers at all.'

Paul bristled. 'All Rosemary is concerned with are results. She expects her staff to be efficient.'

'And what do *you* expect your staff to do?' Zoe asked crisply. 'Until this morning I thought I was actually employed as your secretary. Quite obviously, my duties are expected to extend further than just that.'

Paul fought back his rising irritation. He was genuinely sorry for what had happened that morning, but she didn't have to keep rubbing salt into the wound. 'Yeah, well, I'm sorry...'

Zoe waved the apology away. 'Save it.'

'Point taken.'

'May I make a telephone call?' Zoe asked.

'Sure,' Paul replied unsuspectingly. 'Go ahead.'

'Thank you.' Zoe began to dial. 'Hello, Jim,' she said a few moments later as the call was answered. Paul tensed. With an effort he kept his face impassive as he studied the file on the desk in front of him. 'Yes, it's Zoe... How's Lucy?... Oh, terrific.' There was a pause, then, 'I beg your pardon? Oh no, well, look, I won't hold you up. I was just wondering if we could have dinner somewhere tonight.' Paul experienced some grim satisfaction at the disappointment in her voice; from the sound of it his father was actually fobbing her off. 'Oh well, not to worry,' Zoe said with a brightness that was obviously forced. 'No, no, if you're busy, you're busy... Yeah, okay, see you soon.'

'Father playing hard to get, is he?' Paul smiled sweetly across the desk at her. 'Or has he just lost interest?'

Zoe threw the pencil she was holding down onto the desk angrily. Clearly, she was very put out by Jim Robinson's rejection of her.

But if Paul had thought, hopefully, that that was the end of the relationship, he himself was soon to be disappointed. If Jim had been too busy to go out with her on that occasion – and there had been the worry of Lucy as well – there soon came a time when he wasn't too busy. When Paul learned a few days later that his father had taken Zoe out to dinner, he was dismayed.

'Gran, aren't you worried about Dad?' he asked Helen that same evening.

'Why should I be worried about him?'

'I mean he's making a fool of himself over Zoe.'

'Really?' Helen raised her eyebrows. 'How's that?'

'Oh come on,' Paul said. 'She could be his daughter.'

'But she isn't,' helen quietly pointed out to him. 'How old is she?'

Paul thought for a moment. 'Twenty . . . twenty-one.' It couldn't be much more than that; Zoe was very young.

'Paul, your mother was married with two children by the time she was twenty-one,' Helen said gently. 'Zoe is an adult.'

But only just, Paul thought. 'Do you know what I think?'

'What's that?'

'I think my father's going through the male menopause.'

Helen smiled. 'I hope he doesn't hear you say that,' she said. She shook her head. 'Male menopause indeed.' Her smile faded. 'All right, I know Zoe is younger than your father, but if he wants to take her out, that's none of our business.'

Paul thought it was. 'If he makes a fool of himself it reflects on the whole family,' he said emphatically. 'God knows what Lucy and Scott think of it.'

'They probably respect your father's privacy,' Helen said shortly. 'As I suggest we all should.'

But if Helen was inclined to dismiss it so easily, or at least to make a show of doing so – perhaps she did have her own worries about it – Paul was unable to do so. As long as his father and Zoe continued to see each other, Paul foresaw the danger of the family being torn apart because of it. He could tell that Lucy, in particular, felt threatened just because her father had taken it into his head to start behaving like a teenager again. He was being downright selfish as far as his family was concerned. Until now, Paul had always admired his father's commitment. Even if they'd had their ups and downs in the past, Paul had always respected his father for that.

Matters came to a head during the long Easter weekend when Zoe accidentally broke Lucy's pet egg. Lucy was most upset; she had been looking after that egg for weeks. She had nursed it and comforted it; she had spoken to it; she had christened it Eggward. To her, that simple brown, slightly speckled ovoid was not just an egg; it was a living creature that needed constant love and attention. She had picked up the idea from her cousin Nikki who had brought her own egg home as part of a school assignment that had something to do with parenthood.

The family had been on a picnic. It had been a marvellous day, only to be spoilt for Lucy. It started when her father went out again shortly after they had returned to the house. Helen had cooked a roast dinner for them; Lucy had pouted and refused to eat until her father was sitting in his customary place at the table. Helen had told her not to be silly; Paul had sympathised with his little sister.

They were still at the table when Jim walked in with Zoe, which Paul thought was pretty brazen. Much to his disapproval, Helen insisted she join them for dinner; there was plenty of food, she said, more than enough to go round. She fussed; Lucy began to pick desultorily at her food; Paul wasn't hungry.

'So where have you been, Dad?' he asked.

With more brighteness than Paul felt was necessary, Zoe answered. 'Oh, we went for a walk.'

Lucy lowered her fork. 'What for?'

'We just went for a walk.' Jim looked ill at ease.

'Sounds exciting,' Lucy observed with some wryness.

Zoe laughed. 'It wasn't so bad.'

'I thought we should conserve our energy for tonight,' Jim remarked.

'What?' The disappointment showed in Lucy's eyes. 'You're not going out *again*? Why? Where?'

Jim turned to Zoe. 'I thought we might go to Lassiter's. Okay?'

Lassiter's was the new hotel complex further along the main road. It had everything, including a disco with flashing lights and a loud band. Once more, Paul thought sourly, his father was out to make a fool of himself.

'That sounds great,' Zoe said with a smile.

After dinner, they sat in the living room. Lucy was on the floor in front of the television set, watching one of her favourite cartoon shows. Beside her, nestling in a cardboard box packed with cotton wool, was her egg. Jim and Zoe were on the settee; Paul and Helen were seated opposite them. Jim was trying to make conversation, but wasn't finding it easy above the volume of the television.

'Please, Lucy,' Helen said. 'Turn that down a bit, will you.'

Grudgingly, Lucy reached forward and turned the volume down a fraction. But it was still loud; the cartoon characters capered across the screen; Jim was still trying to talk.

'Oh, for heaven's sake, Lucy,' he said finally in exasperation. 'Turn it off.' Lucy ignored him; Jim's voice sharpened. 'I said turn it off.' Lucy scowled at him, then with undisguised ill-grace; did as she was told. 'I couldn't hear myself think,' Jim said in the sudden silence.

'I'm bored,' Lucy complained.

'Lucy.' In an obvious attempt to be friendly, Zoe knelt on the floor beside the girl and nodded to the egg in its box. 'Who's your friend?'

'What friend?' Lucy's expression was still sullen.

'The egg.'

'That's not an egg,' Lucy returned. 'That's Eggward.'

'May I have a look at it?' Zoe asked with a smile.

'It's a him – not an it.' Lifting the box from the floor, she held it out to Zoe. The egg wobbled slightly on its nest of cotton wool. 'Be careful.'

'Oh, he's lovely.' Zoe smiled at the object that had been described by Clive Gibbons next door, when Lucy had shown it to him, as not just an egg but a significant piece of shell, protein and albumen that had posed the most vexing questions known to human kind. 'The egg,' he had said in admiration. 'The single unity, the ultimate symbol of fertility . . . Ah, what mysteries are contained in this simple but intricate structure; what a soul is already lurking therein.' Zoe smiled at the egg. 'Hello, Eggward,' she said. 'How old are you?'

'He can't speak.' Lucy looked at her reproachfully. 'He's only a baby.'

'Ah, but a beautiful baby – isn't he, Jim,?' Holding the box aloft, she turned suddenly to show the egg to Jim. The egg wobbled more violently with the abruptness of Zoe's movement, then rolled over the side of the box. It fell to the floor. It shattered; it splattered. 'Oh, Lucy.' Zoe stared down in dismay at the mess on the carpet, at the remains of what, only a second or two before, had been Eggward with a soul. 'Oh, I'm sorry. I didn't...'

Lucy was horrified. 'Eggward!' she wailed, scrambling forward on her knees to pick up the broken pieces of shell. She howled, and the tears streamed down her cheeks. She turned on Zoe, her eyes full of hatred. 'You did it on purpose,' she cried.

Zoe was backing away from her. 'No, no,' she protested. 'I wouldn't do that.'

'Yes, you would,' Lucy screamed, her face contorted with rage. 'You're a mean, horrible person. I hate you.'

Reaching forward, Jim grabbed his daughter before she had time to attack Zoe physically, and held her against him. 'Lucy, don't talk to Zoe like that,' he commanded. 'It was an accident. These things happen.'

Zoe was on her feet. Paul glared at her. 'See what you get for interfering,' he said tightly.

Helen was clearing up the mess on the floor. 'We'll get you a new one, darling,' she promised her granddaughter.

But Lucy was not to be mollified. 'That was Eggward,' she whimpered. 'No egg's the same.'

'I know.' Jim was cradling Lucy's head against his shoulder, comforting her in her misery. 'I know.'

Zoe looked stricken. 'Maybe I should go home,' she suggested unhappily.

Jim took Zoe home. Helen was still cleaning up. 'She's a mean and horrible person,' Lucy said viciously. 'And I'm never going to talk to her again.'

Helen straightened. 'Can we forget about this, please,' she said with a sigh.

'Forget about it?' That was something Paul was not prepared to do.

'Paul, it was an accident.'

'Well, it wouldn't have happened if she hadn't been here,' Paul muttered.

'She's feeling bad enough as it is,' Helen said crisply. 'You don't have to make it worse.'

But Paul didn't care *how* bad Zoe felt. She had not only wrecked Lucy's egg, but she was wrecking their home as well.

When Jim returned to the house, Paul immediately challenged him. 'Well? What did you come back for? To see how much damage you've done?'

They were alone in the living room. Lucy had been sent to bed; Helen was in the kitchen. 'I imagine you're fairly pleased with yourself,' Jim said gruffly.

'Don't blame me, Dad,' Paul said. 'You brought this on yourself.'

Jim's expression was stony. 'I'd like you to apologise to Zoe first thing in the morning.'

Paul gestured angrily. 'Like hell I will.'

'This may come as a surprise to you,' Jim snapped, 'but that wasn't a request. This is still my house.'

'Which doesn't exclude me from having an opinion.' Paul faced his father. 'I've got eyes, you know, and what I see is a man making a fool of himself.'

'Watch it, Paul.'

'Well, you *are*,' Paul cried. 'You're not only old, but you're stupid as well.'

Jim raised his hand; he brought the back of it sharply across Paul's face. Paul reeled backwards, and from the doorway, Lucy, who had heard and seen it all, screamed. 'Oh, no, Daddy! Daddy! No!' She rushed between her father and brother. 'No, please don't!' There were tears in her eyes.

The tension in the room was almost unbearable. Paul's head was still ringing from the force of the blow. He wiped the back of his hand across his mouth. A small smear of blood trailed across his fingers. He stared at his father with hostility. 'I think I should leave this house,' he said in a strained voice.

Jim nodded. 'If you think that's best.' His face betrayed no emotion.

'No, Paul, no,' Lucy sobbed desperately. 'Daddy, you don't really want him to leave do you?'

'Yes, I do.' He looked suddenly disconcerted. 'You must try to understand, sweetheart.' He attempted to put a comforting arm around her, but she pulled away from him.

Also concerned about the effect this family conflict might have on her, Paul tried to reassure his sister. 'Lucy, I do think it's best that I should go.'

Lucy shook her head in abject misery. Helen hurried in from the kitchen. 'What on earth is going on?'

Lucy rushed to her. 'Daddy hit Paul,' she cried brokenly. 'And now Paul's going to leave.'

Helen stared disbelievingly at Jim, then at Paul. She turned back to her son-in-law. 'Jim?'

'And it's Easter, too,' Lucy wailed.

Paul turned away. 'I'm going to pack my bags,' he announced flatly.

Lucy followed him into his room. 'Don't go, Paul,' she pleaded.

Paul fought back his own rising emotion. He smiled sadly at his sister. 'Now come on, don't get all miserable on me,' he said with a forlorn attempt at cheerfulness. 'It's time I left home, anyway. I'm a big boy now, you know.'

Despite all her unhappiness, Lucy managed a watery smile which was gone just as quickly as it had appeared, to be replaced by a frown. 'But fighting with Dad!'

Gently, Paul began to stroke her soft, silky hair. 'Just because people fight,' he said quietly, 'it doesn't mean that they don't *care* for each other. Look at Max and Danny next door. If they went for a whole day without having an argument you'd wonder what was wrong – wouldn't you?'

'Yes, but Max never hits Danny.' The logic of that was irrefutable. Paul fell silent. 'Anyway,' Lucy said with a new confidence, 'I'm going to make Daddy ask you to stay.'

Paul was touched by her fervour. He smiled again. 'It's best you keep out of it, Lucy,' he said fondly. 'You don't really understand what's going on between us.'

'I'm just a little kid, aren't I?' Lucy regarded him with a hurt expression. 'Who doesn't understand anything.'

'That's not what I'm saying.'

'Well, I know a lot more than you think, Paul,' she said, turning to the door. 'I know that we're the only family you've got.'

Paul stared thoughtfully after her. There were times when she quite surprised him by her maturity, when she didn't seem like a little girl at all.

But his mind was made up; there was no way he could be persuaded to change it. When he had packed a bag, he called the Lassiter Hotel and booked a room. It would be expensive, but he could afford it – and, anyway, he intended to remain there only for as long as it took him to find a more suitable place.

'This is such a shame, Paul,' Helen said sorrowfully, as she put down the tray she had just brought into the living room from the kitchen. On the tray were three steaming cups of Milo. 'Would you like a hot drink before you go?'

'No thanks, Gran.'

Lucy was staring at him with desperation in her eyes. Scott looked up from his textbooks which were spread over his father's desk in the corner. 'You have brought this on yourself, you know,' Helen said reproachfully.

'Yeah.' Paul shrugged. 'Well, I suppose I'm better off out of here, anyway.'

'Where are you going to stay?' Helen asked him.

'I've booked a room at Lassiters.'

'But what's that going to prove?' Helen shook her head uncomprehendingly. 'Throwing money away on a fancy hotel?'

Lucy moved across the room to Paul and clutched his hand. 'Don't go, Paul,' she begged in a small, plaintive voice. 'I don't *want* you to go.'

Paul placed his arm around her waist and gave her a comforting squeeze. 'Come on, Lucy, it's all right. I have to go.'

Scott stood up and advanced on Paul with outstretched hand. 'Good luck, mate,' he said earnestly.

'Yeah. Thanks.' Paul shook his hand.

'Sorry to see you go.' Scott glanced at Helen. 'I still say Dad's in the wrong.'

Helen frowned at him in disapproval. 'I don't think any of us have the right to undermine your father's authority,' she said.

It was time to leave. Paul embraced his grandmother. 'See you, Gran.'

Her eyes were misty. 'Take care, Paul.'

Lucy was on the verge of tears again. Paul gave her another hug. He tried to sound cheerful. 'Hey, hey, come on. I'm not going to South America. I'm going to be here so often that you'll soon get sick of me. After all, I've got to have *someone* to help me paint the town red.' He released his sister. 'I'll see you.'

Scott walked with him to the front door. Behind him, Paul heard Lucy's sobs. 'I *hate* Daddy,' she was crying. 'I hate him.'

The hotel room was comfortable, but impersonal. There was room service and a swimming pool. There was a restaurant and an arcade of shops. But it was still the holiday weekend, and the place had a deserted, forlorn air about it.

Zoe Davis found him the following afternoon sitting at one of the tables in the swimming pool area. There was a drink on the table in front of him, but he had hardly touched it. 'Am I interrupting?' she asked, coming up behind him.

'What does it look like?' Paul gestured listlessly to his surroundings. 'I'm not doing anything.'

There was only about half a dozen people scattered among the tables. There was no one in the swimming pool. Zoe sat down opposite him. She looked concerned. 'I know it's my fault that you're here,' she said quietly. 'And I'm sorry. I didn't mean it to happen.'

'Yes, well, it gives me more time to think, I guess,' Paul said glumly. 'See things a little more clearly.'

'I'm sorry,' Zoe repeated. 'That's all I came to say.' She paused. 'And to ask you if you want me to quit.'

'What for?'

Zoe sighed. 'Paul, you're not making this any easier for me. You know what I'm trying to say. I mean, can we continue to work together if I'm going out with your father?'

Paul smiled faintly. 'Don't mix your personal life with business. That's what I keep telling you.'

'So?' She was watching him expectantly. 'What does that mean? Do you want me to stay, or do you want me to go?'

'It's up to you,' Paul told her. 'As far as I'm concerned you're a very efficient secretary.'

'There are other people – better people.'

Paul was toying with his drink. 'Do you want to go?'

'Do you want me to go?' Zoe countered.

Paul felt himself cornered. 'No,' he said quietly.

'Then we'll leave things the way they are then,' Zoe said with a relieved smile.

'Okay.' Paul was unhappy. He had just committed himself, and hadn't made things easier for himself. Zoe stood up. There was something else Paul needed to know. 'Zoe, this thing between you and my father – is it serious?'

She hesitated. 'What do you mean – serious?'

'Serious. Two hearts beating as one, moonlight and flowers – true romance.'

'Do I love him – is that what you mean?'

'Yes.'

There was another brief hesitation. 'Yes, I do,' she said finally.

'I see.'

They stared at each other. Paul tried not to show his bitter disappointment. 'I've caused enough trouble in your family, Paul,' Zoe said a little sadly. 'There's you – and Lucy. She won't talk to me; she's hostile. I tried to make things up with her, you know, but she slammed the door in my face.' She shook her head slowly. 'I won't do anything to make it worse.'

But it did become worse. Perhaps Zoe really had tried; perhaps she had really meant what she said - but whatever efforts she did make were certainly not helped by the weekend she spent with Jim in the country.

For Jim it was a business trip. When Helen came to the office that day and told him that Jim would be away for that weekend, Paul had immediately put two and two together. He looked sharply at Zoe who suddenly busied herself by putting on the jug for coffee. She had already told him that she would be unable to work on the report that needed to be completed by Monday because she was going away that weekend.

Helen had dropped in to the office to invite Paul home for dinner that night. Paul had hedged; Helen had been determined to do some fence-mending. 'Oh come on, Paul,' she had insisted. 'You have to break the ice some time. He *is* your father.'

Paul had finally given in. But it was inconvenient for him that same night, he had said; he needed to work on the report. 'What about tomorrow night?' he had suggested. Tomorrow was Saturday.

'That's no good,' Helen had said ruefully. 'He won't be there? He's going away for the weekend.'

From that time on, as Paul was later to learn, Lucy declared total warfare. She did everything in her power to disrupt the relationship between her father and the woman, the stranger who was claiming so much of his affection. When they were together in Jim's house, she interrupted them with any flimsy excuse that came to mind. One night, she tipped a glass of water over Zoe. She pretended it was an accident, that she had stumbled - but it was quite obvious to everyone that she hadn't. Zoe was saturated, and Jim was livid. Catching hold of

Lucy, he bent her over his knee and gave her a hiding. Lucy howled and howled – and swore immediate revenge. What had started out as a perfect evening was left in a shambles.

For the first few times, when Zoe's office telephone rang and there was no response at the other end when she answered it apart from a click as the line was disconnected, she put it down to a wrong number. But then, as the calls kept coming, she became increasingly exasperated. She complained about them to Paul who told her not to worry; it was probably some fault at the exchange. Then she began receiving the calls at home. 'It's weird,' she said. 'It's crazy. Whoever it is, hangs up when I answer.'

'Perhaps it's an old boy friend,' Paul suggested.

'Oh.' Her face clouded, then she shook her head. 'I don't think so.' But all the same her expression remained uncertain.

'If it *is* some sort of a freak,' Paul said, 'he's bound to give up sooner or later. It's generally the way.'

'I hope so,' Zoe said fervently. 'It's giving me the willies.'

But the telephone calls were still coming. They were getting worse. Now there was heavy breathing at the other end of the line. 'Why don't you get yourself a whistle?' Paul suggested. 'The next time this person calls just blow the whistle in his ear. You'll never hear from him again.'

'That's an idea,' Zoe said thoughtfully.

The following evening, Helen and Jim were startled to hear a sudden thump in the hall, then a scream. There were more screams interspersed with violent sobbing. They ran into the hall from the living room to find Lucy lying on the floor, holding her head in both hands and in obvious pain. The telephone receiver was dangling freely and the stool beside the telephone table had fallen on its side.

Jim scooped Lucy up in his arms. Helen picked up the telephone receiver and held it to her ear briefly, and hearing nothing replaced it. Lucy was still screaming.

Once again, Clive was called in from next door. Lucy complained of a constant ringing sound in her ears. 'She keeps talking about being hurt by the telephone,' Jim told Clive. 'But she definitely hit her head hard when she fell off the stool.'

Examining her, Clive discovered that she had a ruptured eardrum. He wasn't surprised that she was in so much pain.

'Does that mean permanent damage?' Helen asked anxiously.

'Not if it's treated properly,' Clive told her. 'But bangs on the head can be pretty tricky. There could be concussion.' He closed his bag. 'I want her to go straight to hospital.'

In the morning, when she arrived at the office, Zoe looked quite pleased with herself. 'Well, that should have done it,' she said as she moved behind the desk and sat down.

'What should have done what?' Paul asked.

'The whistle idea. I blew it as hard as I could. It would have given him a fractured eardrum at least. I hope so, anyway.'

Paul stared at her. Suddenly, things were falling into place. He already knew about Lucy's accident. Helen had called him to tell him about it. 'What time was this?' he demanded thickly.

She looked at him strangely. 'I don't know. About seven, I guess. Why?'

'Lucy.'

'Oh?' She was suddenly wary.

'A fractured eardrum. She's in hospital.'

'My God! How is she?'

'They think she'll be all right. She needs to be kept under observation for a while. Jim's with her now.'

'I didn't know,' Zoe whispered. 'How *could* I know?' She shook her head slowly in bewilderment. 'But *why*?'

Zoe looked so young and confused that Paul felt genuinely sorry for her. 'She was only trying to keep the family together,' he said gently.

Rising to her feet, Zoe moved across to the filing cabinet. 'Jim asked me to marry him, you know.'

Paul nodded. 'I thought something like that might have been in the air.'

Zoe sighed. 'We talked and talked. I finally agreed.'

'I didn't know that.'

'But now . . .' There were tears in Zoe's eyes. 'I don't know. I don't think I can. All this trouble. Lucy will always hate me. She must have been desperate.'

'She was very unhappy.'

Zoe shook her head. 'No, I can't blame her. She was fighting for something she loved.'

'And you?'

'I don't think so,' she replied sadly. 'I don't think I have the strength.' Her lips trembled; the tears welled in her eyes. 'I . . . I honestly don't know, Paul.'

Four

It wasn't as if a Japanese restaurant was the worst place they could have chosen; it could have been a Malayan restaurant, Mexican, Mongolian, or Javanese – the result would have been exactly the same. Max would still have managed to put his foot in it some how.

It was a long weekend, and of course Max had to find something to beef about. This time it was the garden hose. 'Typical, isn't it?' he grunted as he struggled with one of the connectors. 'Made in Taiwan.' He grimaced in disgust. 'I might have known it.'

Madge was hanging up a wash. 'I don't see why you want to water the garden, anyway, after all the rain we've had.'

'It's Saturday.' Max looked at his sister as if she weren't quite all there. 'I always water the garden on Saturday.'

'All right, all right.'

Noticing Danny, Max called to him. 'What have you been doing with the hose?' he demanded.

'Nothing.'

'Then how come the thread's all screwed up?'

'What's that got to do with me?'

'Because you, my lad, were the last to use it.'

'I wasn't.'

'Yes you were.'

'No I wasn't.'

'May I say something?' Madge called across from the washing line where she had just hung up one of Max's shirts.

'No, you may not,' Max snapped at her.

'What's the big deal, anyway?' Danny queried. 'You're a plumber; you can fix it.'

'That's not the point.' Max was quite red in the face. 'And don't give me none of your lip.'

Why was there always this bickering? Danny felt down enough as it was. 'I haven't touched the damned thing!' he yelled. 'Can't you get that into your head? It's always the same with you. You've always got to blame somebody for *something*. I'm fed up.' He stormed back into the house.

He *was* fed up – totally and utterly. It was always the same. The family was drifting apart. They didn't seem to do things together any more, and it had been like that since his mother had walked out on them. And there was Max's constant harping on about things. No wonder Danny was feeling depressed.

'Do you have any plans for the long weekend?' Madge asked him. She was sitting on the other side of the kitchen table, shelling peas.

'No,' Danny replied gloomily.

She looked up at him sharply. 'What is it, Danny? What's the matter?'

'Nothing.'

'I see.'

Danny relented. Yes, there was something on his

mind. He had just made up his mind to tell her what was troubling him when Max tramped dejectedly into the kitchen. 'No good,' he growled. 'I'll just have to buy a new one.' He glared reproachfully at the connector he was holding, then dropped it into the rubbish bin. He rubbed his hands together. 'Right now, what's for lunch?'

'Scrambled eggs,' Madge told him.

Max frowned. He looked at his sister with her bowl of peas. 'What about the peas?'

'They're for dinner.'

Danny had an idea. His expression brightened. 'Look, seeing that none of us have got any plans,' he said, 'why don't we do something together?'

'What a nice idea,' Madge said enthusiastically.

Max was regarding his son with suspicion. 'Like what?'

'Oh, I don't know.' Danny thought for a moment. 'We could go to the Art Gallery,' he suggested. 'There's a modernist exhibition.'

Max snorted. 'I'd rather watch Madge cut her toenails.'

'Oh charming,' Madge groaned.

'It could be interesting,' Danny said. 'The exhibition, I mean.'

'Strewth,' Max said with a grimace. 'Half of 'em could have been done by a chimp with a spray gun.'

'Oh,' Danny cried out in frustration at his father's grossness. 'You . . . You're such a philistine.'

Max was outraged. 'You just watch your mouth,' he bellowed. 'I'll have you know my famous forefather –'

'Was a deck hand on the *Endeavour*,' Danny finished for him. It was an old story. Danny had heard it at least a thousand times.

'Can't you two do anything but fight?' Madge placed the bowl of peas on the table.

'Apparently not,' Danny answered.

'Yeah, well.' Max looked at them both with an air of self-vindication. 'It's better than not talking at all.'

Danny had to accept that. 'Yes,' he said.

Max nodded. 'Right.'

Danny nodded, too. 'Right.'

After lunch, Danny helped his aunt with the washing up. He was still feeling despondent. 'We could still go to the Art Gallery,' Madge proposed, then looked at him with a sympathetic expression. 'You really wanted to go with your father, didn't you?'

Danny shrugged. 'It might have been fun.'

'Why don't you invite Nikki and Scott over for the afternoon?' Madge suggested. 'They're your friends, aren't they?'

It wasn't as easy as that. 'I guess I just don't fit in with them any more.' He had been feeling so much out of things lately. He wished more than anything that he could explain to her exactly how he felt.

Madge took the tea towel from him and draped it over its rack. 'I know it's a difficult time,' she observed quietly. 'Nobody adjusts easily to a complete change of lifestyle. I mean, now that you're working at the bank. A new job, new responsibilities.'

'I don't know if it's so much that,' Danny mused unhappily. 'Maybe it's me that's different.'

'But from what I've heard,' Madge said, 'you were very popular at school. What happened to those friends?'

Different paths, new interests. Danny sighed. 'I guess I don't belong any more.'

Madge was looking quite concerned. 'But Danny, your family – us – surely, *we* don't make you feel that way?'

'It's not that.'

'What is it then?'

'Well.' He fished for the right words. 'Well, I miss Mum . . . sometimes . . . and Dad . . . I just can't . . .' He shook his head woefully. 'Oh, I don't know.'

Although he felt he had made a botch of it, he must have imparted at least something of what he had felt to her. How exactly she had gone about broaching the matter to Max, Danny didn't know. But talk to him she had. As a matter of fact, they were still talking about him when Danny came out of his room later that afternoon. He could tell by the sudden silence, by Max's assumed nonchalance and the bright way in which Madge hurried towards him.

'Danny, guess what?' she greeted him enthusiastically. 'Your father has kindly offered to take us all out for dinner tonight. Restaurant of your choice as well.'

Danny was delighted. All of them, the whole family! He grinned at Madge, then at his father who was now looking a little abashed. 'Oh, good one,' he said. He thought he knew just the place.

The restaurant was Japanese and comparatively new. Max grumbled a little when he learned he would have to take off his shoes. He looked doubtfully at the sushi.

'Hey, I can't eat this,' he complained loudly. 'It's raw.' He called to the waiter. 'Hey, garçon.'

Madge nudged him forcefully in the ribs. 'Max, for heaven's sake!'

'It's *supposed* to be raw,' Danny told him. 'It's sushi. It's a great delicacy.'

Max studied the delicacy critically. 'I don't like the look of it all the same,' he said.

Shane had brought Daphne along. Things were beginning to look quite serious between them. 'Max, why don't you try the teriyaki?' she suggested.

Max peered into the bowl she had passed to him across the table. 'Well, at least it's cooked,' he observed. He pushed the sushi towards her. 'Here, swap.'

There was inscrutability and soft movement all around them. Shane poured his brother a glass of wine. Danny silently toasted him. 'Max, please,' Madge said worriedly. 'Try not to make a spectacle of yourself.'

'Yeah. All right.' It was clear to everyone that Max was not feeling at ease in the Japanese restaurant. 'I'm sorry.'

'How are you going, Dad?' Shane asked after some moments. 'Enjoying yourself?'

Max was tentatively sampling the teriyaki. 'Fine,' he said with an obvious effort. 'Very nice. Yes, very nice.'

'I'm so glad you could join us, Daphne,' Madge said.

Shane slipped an arm possessively around her. 'Well, she's almost one of the family now.' He winked at Danny.

Danny was helping himself to some more food. 'Would you like some, Dad?' He indicated the bowl.

'What is it?'

'Squid.'

'Is it cooked?'

'No.'

Max shook his head, then looked momentarily wistful. 'What I wouldn't give for a plate of steak and chips with an egg on top . . .' Madge nudged him again. Danny was holding out a piece of squid to him between his chopsticks. 'Well, yes, I'm sure the squid's very nice, but...' Madge gave him a fierce look. He took the piece of squid and chewed. 'Ah, very nice,' he said unenthusiastically, washing it down with a mouthful of beer.

By the time they finished their meal, Max was quite expansive. He was drinking sake. 'Here we go,' he said, raising the small bowl in which the drink had been brought to him.

'Oh, Max,' Madge said disapprovingly.

Max gave her a puzzled look. 'It's only sake, isn't it.'

Shane patted his stomach and surveyed the empty bowls. 'It certainly doesn't look much,' he observed with a satisfied smile. 'But, hell, it certainly fills you up.'

'And it's delicious,' Madge said.

'I hate to think what my stomach's going to feel like in the morning,' Max said wrily. He smiled. 'Still and all, we had a great time. That's the main thing – eh, Danny?'

Danny agreed with him. He was feeling very pleased. A family occasion, all of them together; it had been so long since the last time. 'It's been a terrific night,' he said happily. 'I really appreciate it.'

The waiter passed the table at which they were sitting without their shoes. Max hailed him. 'Give us the bill, will you, son.'

The waiter nodded blandly and moved on. Daphne reached for her purse. 'Here, let me.'

Magnanimously, Max waved the offer away. 'No way,' he said. He turned to Madge. 'I bet you didn't think we could do it – eh, Madge?'

'What's that, Max?'

'Get on so well for a whole night.'

'Oh yes.' Madge smiled broadly. 'I'm impressed.'

The waiter brought the bill and silently, impassively handed it to Max. Max looked at it. He exploded. 'Hey!' he roared. 'What's this? One hundred and sixty bucks? That's daylight robbery.' Shane tried to silence him, but Max was already in full cry. 'If my shoes aren't out there,' he threatened, 'I'm going to call the cops quick smart.'

'All right, Max,' Madge said with a quick nervous glance around at the other diners who had stopped eating and were staring at them. 'Calm down.'

Max reached for his wallet. He was still smouldering. 'Let 'em off the hook for Pearl Harbour,' he muttered, 'and this is the thanks you get.'

'Don't forget to leave a tip,' Danny said.

Max shook his head firmly. 'No way.' He counted out the money from his wallet, and together with the bill, handed it to the waiter. 'There you go, son. One hundred and sixty bucks. And the only tip you'll get from me is . . . lower your prices, or go out of business.'

'Dad,' Shane protested. He looked up at the waiter whose imperturbability remained quite intact. 'He's only joking.'

'That's right,' Danny said, taking out his own wallet with the intention of giving the waiter a tip.

Max stopped him. 'No way,' he said gruffly. 'Sorry, son, but this place is what you call a rip-off. If you can't see that, then you need your head read.'

A few moments earlier Danny had been feeling quite pleased – now his father was ruining it all. 'If there's any rip-off being done here,' he exclaimed bitterly, 'it's by you, Dad. I suppose you can't help it.' He stood up. 'I'm sorry about this, Daphne.' Dejectedly, he began to walk towards the entrance.

'Hoy, Danny.' Max called after him, then saw that Shane and Daphne were staring at him with disapproval. 'Well, what are you staring at?' he demanded.

'They're staring at you,' Madge said coldly, 'because if they ever have any children they want a reminder of how not to treat them.'

With the exception of Max, they were all on their feet now. 'Hey,' he cried in an aggrieved tone as they followed Danny to the door, 'I haven't even finished my tea.'

Five

The idea was to attract more customers to the coffee shop. If that could be done, and it could be shown that the business could make a profit, then the owners of the building might have second thoughts about their decision not to renew Daphne's lease when it expired. As Clive Gibbons expressed it, 'All you've got to do is prove to them how dumb they would be to kick you out. Drag in new customers, get your register pinging like a pinball machine. *Shame* them into it.'

Daphne rather liked the idea. 'The more the customers,' she mused, 'the more the building profits.'

'By George, I think she's got it,' Clive said triumphantly.

But the next question was, how? 'What you need,' Clive said, 'is a really good publicity campaign.'

That much was obvious. 'I don't know if I could afford that,' Daphne demurred.

'Then what about a contest of some kind?' Clive suggested. 'It would have to be centred around food.' He thought for a moment. 'How about we get someone in to eat something really weird?'

Daphne looked at him. 'Like what?'

'Like a bike.' Clive was warming to the theme.

'A bike?'

'You mean – *eat* a bike?' Scott Robinson asked in wonder.

'Why not a bike?' Clive countered. 'There was a guy in France not so long ago who ate a pushbike. It took him two weeks.'

'To live or die?' Daphne queried.

'Did that include the tyres?' Scott asked.

'And the tubes,' Clive replied with a nod. 'Just think – for two weeks you could have this whole place stacked out with people watching someone devour a BMX.'

'I'd rather have them eating my food, thank you,' Daphne said with a grimace.

They worked on it, going through a number of possibilities. They ruled out baked beans and bananas; chickens and clams were briefly discussed and eliminated; and doughnuts, eels, eggs or frankfurters barely got a look-in. The suggestions kept coming. 'What about a Great Gherkin Eating Contest?' Clive offered brightly.

'Oh.'

'I could get you a price on gherkins.'

'Everyone would be green after the first half-dozen,' Scott remarked.

Clive was still mulling over the idea. 'I once knew a bloke who ate nearly a kilo in a minute.'

'Clive – must we?' Daphne was looking a little squeamish.

Clive dismissed the gherkins. 'All right then – no gherkins.' He had another idea. 'What about haggis? Get all the Scots in.' He registered their blank expressions. 'No? Eh?' He shook his head. 'No.'

They were working through the alphabet. Hamburgers came next. 'Definitely no hamburgers,' Daphne said flatly.

'Why not? You could knock off twenty or so in half an hour.'

When oysters were mentioned, Daphne shuddered. Meat pies, too, were banished. They were down to the P's. 'Pancakes,' Clive said hopefully. 'They're cheap, small and delicious.'

'And orange juice,' Scott said.

Pancakes and orange juice. It sounded all right; no one had any objection. 'All right then,' Clive said decisively. 'Pancakes it is.'

Clive worked on the details for the contest. 'What we'll do,' he said with enthusiasm, 'is give every customer a ticket for the final draw. We'll pull two tickets out of a hat, and the two lucky contestants and their partners will be in for the finale. What they will have to do is make their own pancakes, squeeze their own juice and then eat them. The ones who do it in the fastest time will be the winners. The prize will be, say, one hundred dollars for the best pancake.'

'And orange juice,' Daphne reminded him.

Maybe we should forget the oranges,' Clive said. 'Let's just stick to the pancakes.'

The news of the pancake-making contest soon got around. In the Ramsay house, Shane talked about it at breakfast. 'The way Clive figures it,' he said, 'all of Daphne's customers would be given a ticket for the big draw. Then in about a week or so all the butts are put into a hat and two are picked out.'

'What?' Max Ramsay, leaning against his chair, had been listening to this in interest. 'Only two?'

'That's right,' Shane replied. 'Then they're both

invited back for a gala pancake-making and tossing competition. The winner gets a hundred bucks.'

Madge was at the stove, frying bacon and eggs. 'How do they choose the winner?' she asked.

'Oh, the fastest and best pancake will win,' Shane told her.

Max was frowning thoughtfully. 'I don't think that ticket system is so crash hot,' he opined. 'I reckon everyone should have a go.'

Danny groaned. 'Yeah, and four hundred pancakes later . . .'

'It doesn't matter,' Max said. 'One man, one pancake.'

'What about the women?' Danny asked.

Max gave his son a withering look. 'Since when have *you* become a feminist?' he demanded.

Danny glanced across at his aunt. 'I think *you* should go in for it,' he suggested.

Madge smiled at him. 'I might just do that, Danny,' she said.

Max looked at her scornfully. 'Oh, the chances of winning don't look so good,' he observed.

'I think it's an excellent way to advertise the coffee shop,' Madge said as she began to serve the bacon and eggs.

In the Robinson house, the pancake-making contest was also a topic of conversation at the breakfast table. 'You know, Gran,' Scott said, 'you should enter Daphne's contest. You're a great cook.'

Helen smiled at him. 'Flattery will get you everywhere,' she remarked.

'But you can toss a pancake, can't you?' Scott asked, a little anxiously.

'Yes, I can toss a pancake.' Helen sighed. 'Yes,' she

said, 'I suppose I *could* have a go.'

A poster for the competition was designed by Clive and placed in the window of Daphne's coffee shop. Tickets were sold. Daphne began to have her doubts about the wisdom of it all. The building had been sold, the lease for the shop would not be renewed, no matter how much custom the competition attracted. It all seemed so pointless. There were times when she became quite depressed about it. 'You let yourself dreams,' she told Clive as they made a list of the ticket-holders and their addresses. 'I guess I imagined a whole chain of shops.' She sighed. 'You work ten, twelve hours a day, your head aches and your feet hurt – but you do it because you think it's going to lead to something. And then.' She shook away the gloom and poised her pen over the list once more. 'Okay, what's the next name?'

Clive peered at the ticket stub. 'Max Ramsay,' he told her. 'God, the whole street's in this competition.' He handed her the stub. 'You know the address.'

There was a big turn-up at the coffee shop on the day of the draw. All the tickets had been placed in a plastic rubbish bin. Behind the counter Madge was selling her home-made pies. Money changed hands; the cappuccino machine hissed and rumbled. 'Dab of colour, pinch of excitement,' Clive observed cheerfully.

From behind the counter Daphne noted with some dismay the arrival of Mrs Mangel, the local busybody and black cloud. She always had something to complain about. There was either too much milk in the coffee, or the sugar in the bowl was damp. 'Do you want me to throw her out?' Shane asked her, tongue-in-cheek.

'I'd love you to.'

'Okay.' Shane began to move in the direction of the

angular woman with the sour expression. Daphne stopped him.

'I'd better close up,' she said. 'It's getting a bit crowded in here.' Coming around from behind the counter, she threaded her way through the crowd to the door.

Danny Ramsay had just arrived. Clive intercepted him. 'You work in a bank,' he greeted him, 'so you're obviously a person of incredible moral fibre who's totally beyond reproach – right?'

'Clive, what are up up to?' Danny asked suspiciously.

'We need you to draw the tickets.'

Mrs. Mangel was hovering nearby. 'I can't,' Danny said. 'I've got nine tickets myself.'

'Well, that's easy,' Clive said airily. 'If your number comes up, we'll have an extra draw. We'll have three winners instead of two.'

Mrs Mangel frowned at him in disapproval. 'That's not fair,' she said. 'You're bending the rules.'

'It's only a bit of fun,' Clive assured her.

Mrs Mangel wasn't convinced. 'It might be fun for you,' she said primly, 'but people with tickets take it very seriously.'

'It's all right,' Danny said with a frown of annoyance. 'If I draw my own ticket, I'll disqualify myself.'

'What could be fairer than that?' Clive beamed at him. 'Good, that's settled.'

Moving back to the other end of the coffee shop, Clive stepped up on to a bench that had been positioned beside his rubbish bin full of tickets. He called for silence. 'The draw will now commence,' he announced. When there was silence, he went on. 'My name is Clive Gibbons. I'm the organiser and master of ceremonies.' There was a spattering of applause and one or two boos. 'So if you need any help at all, just see me afterwards.' He gestured grandly to the rubbish bin. 'As you can see, we are employing the most up-to-date lottery system.' There was some laughter, and Clive bowed slightly in acknowledgement, then pointed to Danny who had moved forward through the crowd. 'And we have Mister Daniel Ramsay, an executive officer, on our staff, to supervise the draw.' He waited for the applause prompted by this announcement to die down. 'As two finalists are to be chosen, there will be two draws. Michael, would you like to proceed.' Mike Young, who was helping Daphne in the coffee shop, had been drawn in to shuffle the numbers around a little. He turned the bin one way, then the other way. Clive gestured towards Danny. 'And Mister Ramsay.'

Danny reached into the bin, and produced a ticket with a flourish. He looked at it. 'Ah, ticket number fifty-six,' he announced.

From behind the counter, Madge squealed with delight. 'It's me! I've got it.'

Danny extracted another ticket from the bin. 'And ticket number one hundred and four.'

Clive consulted his list. 'I see here that ticket number fifty-six is held by Madge Mitchell.' There was more applause and another squeal from Madge. 'And number one hundred and four is held by . . . Max Ramsay.'

Max grinned around him as another round of applause broke out. 'What a coincidence,' Daphne said drily. 'Keeping it in the family.'

Clive was speaking again. 'In accordance with the rules, these two lucky individuals will, on a date to be fixed, engage in mortal combat by cooking pancakes to decide the final winner.'

Now, with an expression that didn't bode well for anyone, Mrs. Mangel was pushing through the crowd. She stopped in front of Clive, looking quite formidable. 'Young man,' she said imperiously, 'I would like to know if the two winners are, by any chance, related to the young man who drew the numbers.'

Clive eyed her sternly. 'I'm afraid, Madam, the judge's decision is final, and no correspondence will be entered into.' He raised his arms in benediction and addressed the crowd. 'Thanks for coming, everybody.'

The crowd began to break up, but Mrs Mangel continued to stand her ground. 'Do you think we've got a problem?' Clive asked Daphne who had just joined him.

Daphne glanced at Mrs Mangel who was now looking quite thunderous. 'I think we've got a problem,' she said quietly.

Max Ramsay was taking it seriously. He was determined to win this contest. He began to teach himself to make pancakes, and made an awful mess in the kitchen. 'If you can turn that muck into a pancake,' Madge said distastefully as she regarded the stodgy contents of the bowl in which Max had mixed his ingredients, 'I'll withdraw from the contest myself.'

Max drew himself up with great dignity. He had put everything into his pancake; he had followed the recipe book assiduously. 'All right then. How much?'

'I beg your pardon?'

'How much are you prepared to bet? It's time you put your money where your mouth is.'

'You shouldn't gamble,' Madge said disapprovingly. 'It's vulgar.'

'All right,' Max said shortly. 'I'll tell you what we'll do. You win the contest and your furniture stays in my house. You lose, it all goes. How about that?'

Madge considered this. 'If I win, my furniture stays and yours goes.'

'Done,' Max said after a brief internal struggle. The lines for battle had been drawn.

But there was more to making pancakes, Max soon discovered, than met the eye. He wasn't finding it easy at all. He decided to enlist the aid of Helen Daniels next door.

'Max, I really don't think...'

'Aunt Madge won't like it,' Danny warned him.

The last straw had come for Max when he had turned on the mixmaster and batter had spurted everywhere, on the walls, the ceiling, the window, the floor, and on Max himself. 'Too bad,' he said tersely. 'I mean, she needs the air letting out of her tyres. And I'm going to do it by winning that contest.' His mind had been made up; hc could still taste the batter on his lips. 'How about it, Helen?'

'Well,' Helen said uncertainly, 'I wouldn't want to do anything to upset Madge.'

'Blow her,' Max snorted. 'I mean, she's got an advantage to start off with.'

'How's that?' Jim Robinson asked.

'Well, she's a woman, isn't she? Learned to cook practically before she could crawl. I mean, she's got it over us all.'

Helen was still doubtful. 'I'd like to help, Max, but, really, I don't think I can.'

Now Jim Robinson was taking Max's side. 'Hang on,' he said to his mother-in—law. 'Hang on. Why not? After all, an athlete is allowed to train before the big event. So what's the difference?'

'Nothing, I suppose,' Helen said hesitantly.

'That's right,' Max chimed in. 'Women's lib. Hah! Women's biff, more like it.'

'That's right,' Jim murmured.

'Yes,' Max cried. 'Ganging up on us, hey? Hey?'

'Yeah.' Jim nodded thoughtfully.

'All right,' Helen said with a resigned sigh. 'You win.'

Max grinned at her in unalloyed delight. 'Oh, you beauty, Helen,' he exclaimed. 'Madge won't stand a chance against us. For once, just once,' he relished the possibility, 'I'm going to make her eat humble pancake.' He laughed happily, already feeling that the contest was as good as won.

The following morning, Max was having his breakfast when there was a knock on the kitchen door and Helen came into the room. She seemed surprised and rather ill-at-ease to find that Max was still there. 'I thought you would have been at work by now, Max,' she said.

Max was chewing on a piece of sausage. 'No. No.' He shook his head and swallowed. 'Listen, I thought I might have my first pancake lesson this morning,' he said. 'If that's okay by you?'

Helen glanced uneasily at Madge whose mouth had just assumed a rather grim set. 'Fine,' she said without any real enthusiasm.

'Great.' Max beamed at her.

Madge gave him a glittering narrow-eyed glance, then turned back to Helen. 'You're not teaching Max how to make pancakes, are you?' she asked in a low voice.

'Too right she is,' Max supplied. 'I'm going to wipe the floor with you.' He laughed confidently.

'Max...' Helen made a fluttering motion with her hand. She was clearly embarrassed.

'I see.' Madge was still looking grim.

'That's what I came to talk about,' Helen told her. 'There's no real problem, is there, Madge?'

'Well, I don't know, Helen,' Madge replied. 'Mrs Mangel is already telling everyone that the draw was rigged. I mean, look at it this way – by teaching Max wouldn't that constitute cheating?'

'Not necessarily,' Helen answered. She drew herself up a little. 'Besides, I don't care *what* Mrs Mangel thinks.'

'That's right,' Max said approvingly.

Madge regarded Helen evenly. 'I really don't think it's a wise decision,' she said. 'You know how people talk.'

'Well, they can mind their own business,' Max snorted impatiently. 'If they can't stand the heat, they can –'

'Look, I'm sorry, Madge,' Helen cut across him. 'But I'll make up my own mind without listening to petty gossip.'

'Very well. If that's the way you feel.'

'Yes, I do.'

The two women stared defiantly at each other. There was tension in the room. 'Good,' Max said affably to Helen. 'So it's still on, is it?'

'Come over when you're ready,' Helen said, turning to the door.

'Right. I'll be over in a jiff.'

But he couldn't make it immediately, as he was called out to a plumbing job a couple of streets away. He sent Shane to the shops to pick up the ingredients for his first lessons in making pancakes. He had already sent him next door with the frying-pan. He would be over as soon as he could, he said.

Helen peered into the large shopping bag Shane had put down on her kitchen table. She began to unpack its contents. 'Icing sugar, brown sugar . . . But we're making pancakes. I have everything we need right here.' She shook her head in bemusement. 'I'm beginning to wonder what I'm taking on with your father.'

Shane chuckled. 'Sounds more like a bunfight than a pancake contest,' he observed.

About an hour later, the front doorbell rang. Helen opened it to find Madge on the doorstep. 'I thought I would use the front door,' she said, 'in case you and your student were cooking.'

'Max just phoned,' Helen told her. 'He's taking a little longer over his job.' She stepped to one side. 'Won't you come in?'

'Thanks.' Madge moved into the hall past Helen who closed the door behind them. 'Actually, I only came over to get my frying-pan. Shane said it was here.'

'Yes, I'm sorry about that.' Helen followed Madge into the kitchen. She indicated the shopping bag on the kitchen table. 'I wonder what could have possessed him to send over all this stuff.'

'Ignorance,' Madge said wrily. 'As a cook he makes a very good plumber.'

Helen handed her the frying-pan. 'You could be in for a surprise.'

Madge looked at her for a long, steady moment. 'I do hope there won't be any hard feelings over all this, Helen.'

'Hard feelings? Why should there be any hard feelings?'

'Well, you really have taken on an impossible task,' Madge said. 'I mean, trying to teach Max to beat me at cooking. Letting him loose in a kitchen is like letting a bull loose in a china shop.'

Helen shrugged. 'We'll see.'

'But if he *does* make a fool of himself,' Madge said, 'and he will, I don't want you to feel badly about it.'

'Why should he make a fool of himself?' Helen countered. 'All he has to do is follow my instructions.'

'I think I should warn you that I have won prizes in one or two cooking competitions back home in Coffs Harbour,' Madge informed her.

'I didn't know that, Madge,' Helen said quietly.

After Max's first lesson, Helen's kitchen had all the appearance of a disaster area. There was flour everywhere, and spilt milk and globs of batter. Helen was still in the middle of cleaning it up when Mrs Mangel appeared through the back door. 'Oh, I see you're in the middle of cooking,' she said.

'Ah, yes.' Helen was embarrassed at being caught out like this. Max had just gone, having been called out on another job. Mrs. Mangel had told Helen that she had met him on the path and that he had said that it was all right to go straight on up, the door was open.

Now Mrs Mangel was sniffing the air. 'What a strange smell,' she said. 'Did something burn?'

'Mrs Mangel, you haven't told me what you want,' Helen said impatiently.

'Oh yes.' Mrs. Mangel gave Helen an uneasy smile. 'I'm sorry, um, Mrs Daniels, it's really none of my business, and we both know how things can become misconstrued when people gossip . . .'

'I don't listen to gossip,' Helen said tightly.

'Ah, but other people do, you see,' Mrs Mangel said with the air of one playing a trump card. 'And what's being said, what some people are saying is that you are teaching a certain party to cook.'

'Max Ramsay?' Helen raised her eyebrows. 'Yes, I am.'

'Oh.' Mrs Mangel seemed suddenly deflated.

'Look, Mrs Mangel!' Helen was fast losing what little patience with the woman that remained. 'What *is* this gossip?'

'Well... do you think it's fair that you are actually *teaching* one of the contestants?'

Helen had an answer for that. 'I look upon it as a coach looks upon an athlete,' she said. 'When the big day comes, he's on his own, win or lose.'

'And people are also saying that this is causing a rift between you and Mr Ramsay's sister.'

'A rift?' Helen was surprised by the way people could take the smallest thing and blow it up out of all proportion. 'Oh, that's an understatement.'

'Really?'

Helen decided to have a little fun at the woman's expense. 'Why – don't you know?' she asked, then shook her head quickly as if she had been just at the point of breaking a confidence. 'No, I can't tell you. But please don't let people think it's just a rift.' Mrs Mangel was listening intently. 'It's terrible,' Helen continued, 'when a grown woman nearly resorts to violence.'

Mrs Mangel was looking at her in surprise. 'But I understood you were such good friends.'

'But what has friendship to do with it when you have to get out there and fight?' Helen appeared suddenly concerned. 'You won't tell anyone about this, will you,

Mrs Mangel?' she spoke confidentially. 'But Mrs Mitchell and I are daggers drawn over this competition.'

Mrs Mangel looked definitely interested. 'No, of course not,' she said quickly as she edged to the door. 'Well, ah, yes, I mustn't keep you, Mrs Daniels. Goodbye.'

'Goodbye, Mrs Mangel,' Helen called after her. She smiled as she wondered how long it would take for the word to spread around the neighbourhood.

Max worked hard on his pancakes. He made them by the stack, and he offered them around – but it seemed that Madge had always made sure that the boys were already stuffed with her own offerings beforehand. He continued to practise: he mixed the eggs and flour and milk; he stirred up a noble batter – but no matter how hard he tried, it seemed that nothing could go right. He was beginning to panic.

He looked glumly at the thick golden slab of pancake in the pan as he prepared to toss it. Madge was watching him with exasperated disapproval.

'Will you stop staring at me?' Max yelped. 'It's making me nervous.' Madge said nothing, but continued to watch him. Max flipped the pan; the slab trembled, it lurched. Max flipped the pan harder. The slab shot up out of the pan, then flopped heavily onto the floor. Madge began to shriek with laughter. 'Shut up!' Max cried in agitation as he began to prepare some more batter.

'Oh, Max, clean it up, will you?' Madge pointed to the mess on the floor. 'It looks disgusting.'

'Yeah, I will. I will.'

When the telephone rang, Max was very short with the caller who had a job for him. 'Look, I'm sorry, mate,' he said impatiently. 'I've got a lot on at the moment.'

'Oh Max, really,' Madge chided him when he slammed down the receiver. 'You shouldn't speak to the customers like that.'

Max rounded on her furiously. 'And speaking of business, I suggest you mind your own,' he snapped.

Madge nodded to the stove. 'I'd watch that pancake if I were you,' she advised him calmly. 'The heat's very high.'

'It's *supposed* to be, isn't it?' Max retorted. A cunning gleam appeared in his eyes. 'Trying to give a bum steer.' He shook his head. 'You're not going to win that way.'

'I don't need to. I'm going to win fairly and squarely.'

'Fair? You? The only time *you* were fair was when you used peroxide.'

'Ho, that's good, coming from the person who cheated me out of the school swimming trophy.'

'Oh yeah?' Max glowered at her. 'And who conned Mum out of Grandma's vase, then, eh?'

'Oh really, Max.' Madge made a gesture of exasperation. 'Sometimes you can be so petty.'

'Pet – *me*?' Max gaped at his sister and bitter rival. 'Petty? Look, I'm a reasonable bloke. You ask anyone around here. I'm *noted* for my reasonableness.'

Madge was looking at the pan on the stove. She pointed to it.

Turning to the stove, Max was aghast to see the smoke rising from the pan; the pancake was close to total annihilation. Max swore, and throwing down his tea towel, hurried across the room to rescue it.

By now, thanks to Mrs Mangel, the word had got around the neighbourhood that there was fierce rivalry between

Helen Daniels and Madge Mitchell over this pancake-making contest. It was discussed over coffee, over back fences, in the supermarket, the butcher's, or over a glass of beer in the evening. However, this rivalry which was the cause of so much speculation, was to become even more immediate with the sudden defection of Max Ramsay.

Maria, his estranged wife, had called him from Brisbane, and he had caught the next available plane. Apparently she was in difficulties of some sort. 'Did Dad say how long he'd be away?' Danny asked Madge at breakfast the next morning.

'He didn't say very much at all,' Madge told him. 'Except that your mother is upset and wanted him to go and see her. Apparently she's been back from Hong Kong for some weeks.'

Shane wasn't impressed; he thought his father must have had rocks in his head, rushing off like that. After all, their mother was the one who had run away with what's-his-name. 'Look, we all knew it wouldn't last. And the moment something goes wrong, what does she do? She rings up Dad to come and rescue her.'

'It would be good if they *did* get back together,' Danny mused.

'Oh, Danny, I wouldn't get my hopes up too high,' Madge said gently. 'Obviously your mother's upset at the moment, but I don't think she'll call off the divorce.'

One outcome of Max's sudden dash to Brisbane was that he wouldn't be back in time for the pancake-making contest. However, he had made provision for that. 'He wants you to take his place as his proxy,' Madge told Helen Daniels.

Helen looked at her in dismay. 'But I can't.'

Madge shrugged off-handedly; it was no skin off *her* nose. 'Oh well, it wouldn't have been much of a contest, anyway. *My* pancakes are hard to beat – even if I do say so myself.'

Helen was stung. 'I haven't had too many complaints about mine,' she said a little stiffly. She thought about it some more, then yielded to the temptation. 'Yes, well, I suppose I *could* stand in for Max,' she murmured. 'It would be a shame for everyone to miss out on all the fun.'

Madge smiled at her, quite poisonously.

There was more practice to be done. Helen made pancakes, and Madge made pancakes. Both houses were full of the smell of them. Both families provided willing guinea-pigs. 'Oh, I couldn't eat another thing,' Shane Ramsay said lazily, patting his stomach.

'You've been over at Helen Daniels' place, haven't you?' Madge accused him. 'Are her pancakes improving?'

'Fantastic,' Shane said with a grin. 'As a matter of fact they were so good that I've over-eaten.'

Madge grimaced. 'They can't be better than mine.'

'To be honest, I can't tell the difference,' Shane said obliviously.

'Oh, really?'

'You could have some real competition.'

'Well, I'd better start practising then.' Madge rose from the table. 'And don't you move,' she commanded. 'I'm going to need you later to test them – so I don't want you going anywhere.'

'I couldn't if I tried,' Shane said with a satisfied smirk.

The interest in the contest was intense. Madge and Helen were running equal favourites. Clive Gibbons was running a book on the outcome. Rather importantly, he addressed the crowd that had gathered in Daphne's coffee shop on the day of the match. After introducing the two contestants, he went on: 'Now, management has spared no expense in obtaining two independent judges. As we all know, teenagers are always hungry, so we have great pleasure in announcing the school captains of Erinsborough High.' There was a cheer from the predominantly young crowd. The school captains smiled awkwardly. 'These two will be judging the contest and giving points out of ten for mixing, style, speed, tossing ability – and last, but not least, taste. So, without further ado...' He gestured dramatically towards the two contestants who, in their aprons, were standing beside the stoves that had been set up at the rear of the shop. 'Cooks, to your bowls – and may the best win.'

The two women worked furiously. They prepared and mixed; people in the crowd craned their necks to see them. Batter flew, spatulas scraped, and fat hissed. The pancakes were tossed high; the school captains tasted and nodded. The crowd held its collective breath. They had come to the final toss. Madge flipped; the pancake turned over in the air and came back down in her pan with a decisive little *plop*. But she was still behind on points. All eyes turned to Helen.

But just as Helen was about to toss the pancake, there was a sudden commotion at the door. Heads turned. With a grim expression, and a fierce glint in her eye, Mrs Mangel was pushing her way through the throng. 'Excuse me,' she said in a loud voice just as Helen tossed her pancake. It went high, somersaulted and came down again, missed the pan and fell onto the floor. There was a groan of disappointment.

'Bad luck, Helen,' Clive said. 'But good luck, Madge.

You're now on even points.' Mrs Mangel drew nearer. The school captains tasted the latest offerings. They chewed and nodded again, then wrote down their findings. Clive took the sheet from them. 'And the winner is – Helen Daniels.'

There was a mighty cheer, and a burst of applause. Helen beamed. Madge offered her congratulations. Mrs Mangel stopped in front of Helen and Madge. 'Excuse me,' she said again.

Helen's face clouded. 'Why should we? When you tried your hardest to ruin everything for me.'

Clive stepped forward and introduced himself. 'I'm in charge here,' he said.

'So if you've got anything to say,' Daphne told Mrs Mangel, 'say it to him.'

'It's perfectly straightforward,' Mrs Mangel said, fixing Clive with a steely gaze. 'I've been to the Council.'

'What for?' Daphne looked at her in surprise.

'Because I believe it was my civic responsibility,' Mrs Mangel replied haughtily. 'The Council inspector will be here shortly.'

'Inspector?'

The crowd was drifting away. 'Surely there's some way we can talk this out?' Clive said.

Mrs Mangel shook her head. 'You've been running an illegal lottery, falsifying competitions and raising the noise level in the street to an unbearable level.'

'What do you mean?' Daphne broke in furiously. 'It's got nothing to do with the Council.'

Clive was looking uncertain about that. 'Better hear her out,' he suggested.

Mrs Mangel glanced over her shoulder. 'Ah, here's Mr Archibald now,' she said with a touch of smugness as a man carrying a clipboard and with a row of pens in his shirt pocket entered the shop. 'He'll tell you.'

'What's all this aobut?' Clive demanded.

Mr Archibald frowned thoughtfully at his clipboard. He pursed his lips and he scratched his jaw. 'Well, there do seem to be a number of breaches,' he said.

'That's ridiculous,' Daphne snapped.

Archibald was still consulting his clipboard. 'Exceeding the licensed number of patrons for a start,' he observed.

Shane Ramsay had just joined them. 'This shop wasn't overcrowded,' he protested. 'There hasn't been a breach of the fire regulations or anything like that.'

Mrs Mangel was looking sternly at the man from the Council. 'Don't forget the other matters we discussed.'

Archibald had the long-suffering air of a man who'd had many exhausting dealings with Mrs Mangel in the past. 'Mrs Mangel, Mrs Mangel,' he said with weary patience. 'Just let me handle this, please.' He turned back to Clive. 'You're also contravening a number of health regulations by cooking out here and not in the kitchen.' He held up his clipboard. 'I have here a list of specific breaches.'

Daphne was watching him with a stunned expression.

'Well?' Clive asked. 'What will happen now?'

Archibald regarded him seriously for a moment. 'Look,' he said, 'the Council has no desire to be hard on anybody. So if you call off the contest I think I can safely promise that no more will be said.'

'No way,' Daphne said flatly.

Helen didn't think it was so important. 'At least you can consider it, Daphne.'

But Daphne was adamant. 'No one's going to tell me

what to do with *my* money.' She scowled at Mrs Mangel. 'You interfering old busy-body,' she said menacingly. 'Why you wanted to poke your nose in here...'

Mrs Mangel took a startled step backwards. 'Just because I have a sense of civic reponsibility,' she gasped, 'that doesn't give you the right...'

'Civic sticky-beaking,' Shane said contemptuously.

'All right.' Clive stepped forward to restore the peace. 'Calm down, everybody.'

'I think we should let Daphne sort it out,' Helen suggested. 'I mean, don't worry about the prize money.'

'It's a matter of principle,' Shane stated.

Daphne stood there with her hands on her hips. 'No one's going to tell *me* what to do, Clive,' she said stubbornly.

'I don't see we have much choice,' Clive said with a nervous glance at the Council inspector.

Archibald looked up from his clipboard with its list of specific breaches against the regulations. 'Then I take it the competition is cancelled?' he asked hopefully. Taking the lack of reply as confirmation, he nodded. 'That's fine.'

With another nod to Mrs Mangel, he turned and walked out of the shop. Mrs Mangel, it seemed, was determined to get in with the last word. 'It doesn't look too good for your next shop, does it?' She smirked. 'You know – gambling, flouting the law. A lot of people don't approve of that sort of thing.'

Daphne was studying her closely, her lips curved into a half smile. 'Is that right?' she said slowly. 'Well, then, I think you've done me a favour.'

'What?' Mrs Mangel's own smile disappeared.

'You're not very well liked around here,' Daphne told

her pleasantly. 'And as soon as people find out that I'm up against you they'll be queuing up to offer their support.'

Mrs Mangel sniffed, and then with as much dignity as she could muster, stalked out of the coffee shop. Shane placed his arm around Daphne and kissed her on the forehead. Daphne smiled, and Clive laughed. Mrs Mangel had been put in her place – for the time being at least.

Six

Eileen Clarke was singing 'Jerusalem', and she was singing it very badly. In the Ramsay house next door, Madge Mitchell winced every time she hit a top note.

Clive Gibbons had taken Eileen under his wing. He was giving her lessons, because he had detected a talent that had escaped everyone else that memorable Sunday morning in church when her voice had soared so powerfully during the singing of 'Amazing Grace'.

After the service, Clive had congratulated her. 'You *are* a dark horse, aren't you?' Eileen had simpered. Clive had continued to enthuse. 'Such talent! Such raw potential! What was it Pavarotti once said? Oh yes. "The voice, she is like an instrument. So much is natural; so much must be learnt. Pass the garlic bread."'

'*Pavarotti* said that?' Madge Mitchell had been incredulous.

'He was hungry,' Clive had remarked. 'Even great opera singers have to eat. But the main thing is,' he said gazing tenderly into Eileen's eyes, 'where there's a voice like yours, there is joy in the heart. The joy must be shared with the world, Mrs Clarke – and we're just the team to do it.'

'We?'

'Trust me.' Clive had placed his hand over his heart. 'Put your vocal chords in my hands. I have a piano and you can practise any time you like. Ah yes, I can see them now, those billboards.' His eyes had become quite misty. 'La Scala, the Met, Covent Garden.'

'Well, I . . .'

But Clive had already moved on from his loflty images of the grand opera. 'Forget the opera. Think about the musical stage.'

'Ah, yes.'

'The hills are alive, Mrs Clarke, and what good is sitting all alone in your room? What do you say? The charge will be a bare minimum.'

The lessons had started. It was a rocky road to Jerusalem, and in the house next door Madge Mitchell stared resentfully at her husband, Fred, who had just arrived unannounced from the North Coast. 'Bring me my arrows of desire!' cried Eileen Clarke from next door as Madge tried to gather her thoughts and grievances towards this man who had walked out on her for a younger woman.

'Where's my little girl?' Fred Mitchell was looking expectantly around the room.

Just then the door opened, and Charlene rushed into the room. She hugged her father. Madge looked on impassively. Charlene had always loved her father. Since she had come down south to stay with them, she had talked incessantly of her father, and of Susan, the girl with whom Fred had gone to live and who was now expecting his child. She was quite unconscious of the pain she was causing her mother.

'Dad, I *thought* it was you,' Charlene exclaimed. 'Why

didn't you tell me you were coming?'

'You'd better sit down,' Madge said listlessly as Eileen Clarke continued her onslaught against the walls of the Holy City. 'If you're staying.'

'Of course he's staying,' Charlene said as her father lowered himself into a chair. 'He's only just got here.'

Madge had written to him, as the financial side of things still needed to be worked out. She felt very bitter towards him. Next door, Eileen stopped singing. Silence filled the room. Madge turned to her daughter. 'Charlene, your father and I have something to discuss.'

Charlene took the hint. She looked momentarily hopeful. 'About getting together again?'

Madge shook her head grimly. There was no way that would happen. She had been hurt so badly, after so many years.

'I can't blame you for being annoyed,' Fred said after Charlene had gone.

'Annoyed?' Madge's expression was set. 'I'm furious.'

Next door, Eileen began to sing 'Green Hills of Somerset'. Fred tried to be reasonable. 'Look, you know as well as I do that there's no point trying to keep a failed marriage together.'

'I quite agree,' Madge said firmly. 'But there are more dignified ways of ending it. You made me a laughing-stock in a town where I lived for twenty years.' The bitterness began to overflow and spill out of her. 'What do you think it's like, Fred? Everywhere you go . . . In the shops, and everyone knows your husband's having an affair. You were the guilty one, Fred and I was the one who was punished.'

Fred was looking slightly abashed. 'I never meant that to happen,' he muttered.

Eileen was apostrophising the English hills. Madge looked scornfully at her unfaithful husband. 'Oh, how could you be so naïve? All the little innuendos about our sex life and how I couldn't possibly keep you interested any more.'

'You made too much of it,' Fed said with a small shrug. 'Small towns are always full of gossip. You and I *know* that wasn't true.'

'Do we?' Fred had always had the habit of jumping to conclusions. He couldn't expect her to do the same. 'You're the only man I ever slept with,' she said. 'And you never told me if I was good, bad or indifferent.'

'Oh come on, Madge.'

Fred was plainly embarrassed. Madge didn't spare him. 'I must have bored you since our wedding night. After all,' she made a stab in the dark, 'she's not the first, is she?'

'No, but . . .' Madge's thrust had struck home. She was indignant. Eileen continued to warble and trill her way along narrow English lanes. 'I'm sorry,' Fred said with a rueful expression. 'I thought you knew.'

Eileen Clarke was scaling the heights, while Fred and Madge were discussing Henry, their son. 'You never had any time for him,' Madge said accusingly. '*I* was the one he knew he could come to if he had a problem.'

'Oh yes, and look where that landed him.'

'Are you saying it's *my* fault that our son's in gaol?'

Charlene had said it was her fault in the course of that bitter fight two days earlier. She had accused her mother of not supporting her brother. But enough had been enough. She couldn't possibly keep on making excuses for him. 'Well, you spoilt him rotten,' Fred said. 'For every ten dollars I earnt, you spent five bailing him out of trouble.'

Madge regarded him stonily. 'Because you wouldn't do anything to help.'

'Oh, he was mummy's boy right from the start,' Fred observed with a sour grimace. 'What hope did I have? I wanted to take him to the football, or camping – or something like that – and you wouldn't let him go. It didn't seem to bother you that I went on my own.'

With hardly a bump in the transition, Eileen had turned from the British Isles to the Far East in her singing tour of the world. Now she was attacking 'On the Road to Mandalay'. Some of her low notes were quite alarming. 'If I had let you get your hands on him,' Madge said, 'you would have broken every bone in his body. You never did have any sense of responsibility. You always were a weak man, Fred. If it hadn't been for my pushing you would still be a parking inspector.'

The flying fishes played, and the paddle steamers chunked from Rangoon to Mandalay. 'Did it ever occur to you that I might have been *happy* with my job?' Fred said, a little plaintively. 'You're so damned selfish, Madge,' he went on when Madge didn't reply. 'You decided what you wanted for me, wanted for our children. And none of us had any say in the matter.'

Madge set the trap nicely for him. 'Are you saying that I'm responsible for getting us where we are today?'

'Yes. Totally responsible.'

'Good.' Madge was suddenly businesslike. 'Then I think you'll find that you owe me rather a lot of money – and I intend to get every penny of it.' She paused to allow this to sink in. 'Every penny, Fred,' she said with quiet but devastating emphasis.

Fred stared at her sullenly. 'I might as well go,' he said with a sigh. 'We're not getting anywhere like this.'

'Well, what did you expect?'

'This isn't like you, Madge.' He shook his head in disappointment as Eileen took a spectacular downward plunge into the shimmering waters of the South China Sea.

Perhaps not, Madge thought. 'How would *you* know what I'm like,' she challenged. 'You were always too busy eyeing off everyone else.'

'Stop it!' Charlene was standing in the doorway, her face pale and pinched with anger. She came into the room. 'You've got no right to speak to my father like that.'

'Charlene, I'll speak to him any way I like.' Madge eyed her daughter coldly. 'He was my husband a long time before he was your father.'

Fred leaned forward in his chair. 'Haven't you got someone you can visit?' he asked Charlene.

'You don't have to put up with this, Dad.'

'Charlene, you can always go and see the Robinsons,' Madge suggested.

Charlene wasn't budging. 'I have every right to know what you two are going to do.'

'Go on,' Fred urged her gently. 'I'll see you later.'

There were tears in Charlene's eyes as she glared at her mother. 'It's no wonder you two broke up,' she choked as she swept out of the room.

'Poor kid,' Fred murmured with a sorrowful shake of his head. It was more than Madge could take.

'What hypocrisy!' she exclaimed. 'You don't care about Charlene. You only care about yourself.'

The fiery sun had set in the Far East. 'What do you

want from me, Madge?'

'Money.'

'I don't have any to give you,' Fred said simply. 'I need it for Susan and the baby.'

That baby again. Suddenly, Fred was presenting himself as a caring father. Hypocrisy – the word flitted through her mind again. 'I don't *care* about your family, Fred. I'm too worried about what to do with the old one.'

Madge was determined. She began to go through his assets with him. She was not about to let him cheat her. 'Nobody's cheating you,' Fred protested. 'Things haven't been too good lately. Susan's not coping well – morning sickness and that sort of thing – and I've had to employ extra staff.'

Madge couldn't recall him having been so solicitous during *her* two pregnancies. 'It didn't stop *me*,' she said with asperity. '*I* worked for you when I was pregnant. In fact, I worked in that business for over twenty years, Fred – and I'm not going to have that girl enjoy the fruit of my labours.'

'You were never short of money,' Fred said defensively.

Once more there was silence from the house next door, but there was a trembling, foreboding quality about it. 'I'm looking out for my rights,' Madge said, 'not expecting hand-outs from you.'

Fred's face was expressionless. He spoke quietly. 'I've given my solicitor a list of the profits you have taken from the business. I'm sure you'll find it's all fair and above board.'

'Fair for you, no doubt. What about me?'

'It's not *my* fault you spent it on Henry,' Fred said. 'He should have been in gaol long ago. If that had happened, he would have had more sense and you would have had more money.'

Eileen began singing again. This time it wasn't immediately recognisable. It might have been a Negro spiritual. Madge's mind was still occupied with business. 'I want the Coffs Harbour house sold and split four ways – between you, me, Charlene and Henry.'

Fred began to object. 'And what are Susan and I supposed to do? Live in a tent?' His jaw took on a determined set. 'And Henry is not getting a penny.'

'He's your son.'

'I washed my hands of him years ago.'

'And now I suppose you want to do the same with Charlene?'

'Charlene wants to be a motor mechanic,' Fred reminded her. 'So why don't you let her?'

That was another argument that had been thrashed out between them. 'It's not what I have in mind for her.'

'You see, Madge,' Fred regarded her sombrely, 'you smother everyone and everything. I don't see why you can't let the kids make their own way in life.'

Madge laughed without a vestige of humour. 'That would be really easy for you, wouldn't it, Fred?'

'Why are you being so difficult?'

'Because of what you did to me.'

'What about me?' Fred asked unhappily. 'Don't *I* rate some kind of consideration?'

'I considered you for twenty years.' Madge told him mercilessly. 'Now all I care about is my childlren – and if you won't face up to your responsibilities, then I'll just have to make sure you do.'

Eileen Clarke had trilled her way through two more numbers, 'Danny Boy' and 'The Pipes of Pan' by the time Madge had finished drawing up her list of assets. She handed it to Fred. 'You've forgotten one thing,' he said after he had examined it. 'Diamond.'

'What diamond?'

'The diamond engagement ring I bought you.'

'Madge was appalled. 'But you *can't* count that.'

Fred indicated the sheet of paper he was holding. 'Well, you've got everything of mine listed here – and you sure as hell didn't pay for it.'

'But you gave it to me.' Madge stared at him in dismay.

'You've never worn it.'

'It's an investment.'

'Precisely,' Fred said with a tight smile. 'I put ten grand into it. *My* money.'

'Well, you're not getting it back,' Madge said firmly.

'Like hell I'm not,' Fred growled. 'I'll go to court if I have to.'

It was a threat Madge could handle. 'You wouldn't want to air our dirty linen.'

'*You* might call it dirty linen, Madge. *I* call it ten grand.'

Madge tried another tack. 'I was under the impression you gave it to me because you loved me.'

'Come on, Madge.' Fred was looking at her incredulously. 'You know it was an investment.'

'Yes. For my old age.'

'You're not old yet,' Fred pointed out. 'You've got plenty of time to make a life of your own.'

Madge wasn't so sure about that. 'Oh, Fred, come on, look at me. I'm over forty. Most of my life has been spent rearing the kids and looking after you. What have I got?'

Fred's expression faltered. Uncertainty was briefly

reflected in his eyes. 'Well, ah, you'll find somebody.'

'Ha! I don't see any twenty-year-old throwing himself at *me*.'

'I've said I'm sorry.'

'And that's supposed to make it all better, is it?' Madge's voice quavered. Next door, Eileen's strengthened; she was singing a lullaby. 'I . . . I have nothing, Fred . . . Absolutely nothing. I've lost my friends . . . my home.' She looked at him bleakly. 'What am I supposed to *do*?'

'You'll cope,' Fred answered quietly. 'Of course you will. You always have.' Oh yes, Madge thought sadly. She had always managed in the past. But now . . . 'There's nothing I can say, is there?' Fred stood up and began to move towards the door. Madge stopped him.

'Fred? Did you ever love us?'

'Of course I did.'

'And me?'

Fred gestured awkwardly. 'Look, Madge, please, don't make things so hard.' He took another couple of steps to the door. 'I'm staying at the hotel up the road. Lassiter's. Call me when you've cooled down.'

It wasn't until after he had gone that Madge gave full vent to her feelings. She began to cry. She hated him. No, she didn't. In spite of everything that had happened, she still loved him. It was all so terribly wrong.

It was because she felt the way she did about him that she was drawn to see him again. Perhaps, if she did see him again, she might finally be exorcised of the spirit of him. Either that, or . . .

She dressed with particular care the following morning before she went to see him at the hotel.

'You're still a good-looking woman, Madge,' Fred

said, as he closed the door of his hotel room behind them and gave her a brief but thoughtful appraisal. 'Would you like a drink?'

It was only just after ten-thirty. 'Don't you think it's a little early?' she queried, then realised immediately that this was not the attitude to take. 'No, thanks. I had a cup of tea just before I left.'

They stood facing each other in the hotel room, the one window of which looked out over the car park. After that initial exchange, the conversation had lapsed. Madge wondered if she hadn't made a mistake after all, coming to see him like this in his hotel room. She had put herself at a decided disadvantage, she felt.

'Charlene came to see me,' Fred said after a while. 'She's pretty upset.'

'It's been very hard on all of us,' Madge observed.

'Madge, please believe me.' He was looking into her eyes, and Madge was feeling nervous. 'I didn't mean to hurt you, or the kids. I suppose it was wrong of me, but I honestly thought that this thing with Susan would just blow over. That maybe we could get together again.'

Madge didn't know what to believe. There were times before when she had believed in his sincerity. 'Oh.'

'You know, Madge, there are times when I wish we *were* still together.'

There was something in the way he said it... 'It's funny,' Madge said softly. 'In spite of everything, so do I.'

Fred smiled at her. 'We had the lot, didn't we?'

Yes, they had. Madge thought so. 'It's a pity it wasn't enough.'

'Yes, it was my fault,' Fred said. 'I don't know what got into me.'

'Middle-age, I think.'

'Oh, I don't feel any different now to how I did at twenty.'

He was still an attractive man; he had always managed to bring out those responses in her which she had been determined to withhold from him. Like now. There was that same feeling now, her body a-jangle and on the point of surrender to his persuasiveness. 'Neither do I,' she whispered.

'We were happy then, Madge.'

They were standing so close to each other that she could feel his warmth, his strength. She turned away, not trusting herself. 'We were the perfect couple,' she said with a wistful smile. 'Everyone envied us.'

'Madge?' She didn't turn back to face him. 'Madge, I'll always love you.'

Oh no. They were the words Madge *didn't* want to hear. It was so unfair. She was trembling. She tried to fight the sweet and quivering weakness that had been triggered by his words, by his proximity in a hotel room where they wouldn't be interrupted. The magic was still there. 'Look at me, Madge.' Slowly, her eyes brimming, she turned to face him. She couldn't help it. She couldn't help anything now. He was smiling at her, tenderly. 'I know you feel the same,' he said.

Afterwards, they went downstairs to the bar. Fred drank a couple of Scotches, and said, 'I didn't think it would turn out like this, did you?'

Yes, the old magic had been there, the old excitement. For a while there, upstairs in Fred's hotel room which overlooked the car park, and with the sun shining in through the window, she had felt so marvellously young again, and in love. Fred had been so tender, and strong, and . . . 'No, of course not,' she replied.

'It's so damned silly, bickering after all we've been through.'

This time, perhaps, he meant it. He had come to a time in life when he could look back over his past mistakes, see where he had gone wrong, and with that knowledge, make sure he wouldn't make the same errors.

Older and wiser, and no more bickering. 'I don't want to fight, Fred,' she said.

He raised his glass to her. 'I'll always hold a candle for you, you know.'

Madge smiled. 'Me, too.' Yes, she was certain now that everything would be all right.

'It was the kids. Always running after them. Charlene this, Henry that. A man began to feel he wasn't needed.'

'You don't need to feel like that.'

Fred brightened. He nodded a couple of times. 'Susan's a good kid.'

It was this mention of the woman who was already carrying his child that made Madge suddenly realise how terribly wrong she had been. She had been labouring under a delusion, and what had happened up there, in his room – well, that was Fred; he hadn't changed; he would never change. Madge suddenly felt numb. Fred was still talking about Susan.

'Not intelligent, mind you, but warm – and I don't mind telling you that I felt a little strange about starting up a family at my age. I mean, a man's not getting any younger, is he? But now I have a whole new future to think about.'

Madge sat there in a daze; she was hardly hearing him now. 'Madge, you can keep the ring,' he was saying. 'Do what you like with it, sell it, keep it for your old age. But I don't want any further claims on me, or the house, or the business – okay?' He glanced at his wristwatch. Madge stared at him blankly. 'Goodness me, is that the time?' He finished his drink, then stood up. 'I'll have to go.' He smiled down at Madge. 'It's been good seeing you, Madge,' he said with a careless wave as he turned away from the table.

For a long time after he had gone, Madge just sat there at the table in the bar of Lassiter's hotel. She saw nothing, heard nothing, felt nothing.

Seven

Any girl would have given her right arm and more to have a date with the muscular and tanned 'Iron Man' Rolf Pertwee, that sporting phenomenon who swam great distances, rode the tumbling waves on a surfboard, sprinted across the sand and jumped the hurdles – in all of which activities, often carried out consecutively, he displayed a stamina that was hardly less than legendary. And not only that, but he was very good looking. He had long blond hair that rippled delightfully in the breeze, and teeth that were strong and flawless. He smiled a lot and endorsed food products with the desirable amount of fibrous content on television. He was a dream. His eyes were blue and clear. He was a bronzed hero built in the classical mode – and tonight he was the prize in that highly popular television show, 'Date with a Star'.

'I love him,' Lucy Robinson said as she settled down to watch the show with Nikki Dennison.

'Oh, he's all right,' Nikki said offhandedly. She didn't want to sound too impressed; she was a few years older than her cousin. All the same, she was watching the screen intently as the compère, a roundish, youngish man in a suit and with a smile that didn't falter, made his introduction.

'Yes, here he is, the man you've all been waiting for – the Iron Man himself.' A welcoming arm was extended. 'Our guest star, Rolf Pertwee!'

The applause was tremendous. The cameras panned, Lucy wriggled, and then there he was, grinning broadly and looking more tanned than ever as he walked out on to the stage wearing a sports coat. The compère shook him warmly by the hand. A few introductory comments were made, there was more smiling, and some more wriggling from Lucy.

'So this time tomorrow night,' the compère was saying to the Iron Man, 'some lucky girl is going to find herself out on a date with you.'

A lucky girl, who would be the envy of all the girls who had missed out. 'Actually, I'm looking forward to it,' Rolf Pertwee said.

There was a barrel that revolved in a frame. In the barrel were the hundreds, perhaps thousands, of entries from the fans out there, who were now, like Lucy and Nikki, sitting in front of their television sets, waiting and hoping. The compère led Rolf across to the barrel. He gave it a couple of spins and grinned at the camera. 'Wait for it, girls.'

Rolf Pertwee's hand disappeared into the opening of the barrel. He rummaged a little; the collective breath was held. After a few moments, the hand was withdrawn. In it was a folded slip of paper. He unfolded it, he peered at it, then looked into the camera. 'The winner is,' he began, then glanced at the paper again, 'Lucy Robinson of Erinsborough.'

There was tumult. The music swelled to a mighty crescendo, lights flashed and changed colour, feet stamped, the compère grinned, and Rolf Pertwee grinned. Lucy squealed and jumped to her feet. 'It's me!' she shrieked. 'It's me! I've *won* it!'

Nikki was stunned. She couldn't believe it. Of all those hundreds, perhaps thousands, of entries. She looked sourly at Lucy who was still jumping up and down in total ecstasy. You little *snake*, she thought.

Now, as his beaming face filled the screen, the compère was addressing Lucy alone. 'And remember, Lucy,' he was saying with impressive sincerity, 'if we don't hear from you tonight, you forfeit your date with Rolf Pertwee. So, please, get yourself to a telephone right away and call us. Right, Rolf?'

'Right,' Rolf said.

Lucy was beside herself with excitement. 'Quick, quick,' she cried. 'I'd better ring up.'

Torn by jealousy, Nikki had been thinking fast. She grabbed Lucy's wrist before she could reach the telephone. 'Hey, hey, you just wait a minute. You *can't* go out with him.'

Lucy looked at her with a puzzled expression. 'Why not? I won the date.'

'You've got to be at least sixteen. It's one of the rules.' It had been on the entry form. Nikki had sent one in herself.

'I look a lot older with make-up,' Lucy said defiantly.

'No, Lucy, you can't,' Nikki told her firmly. 'They won't let you.'

'But I *won* this date.' Lucy was desperate; Nikki was still thinking. 'And once I'm there they can't stop me.'

'But they won't let you go, Lucy. Once they hear your voice on the telephone.'

'Then you can ring up for me.'

'It won't work.' Nikki shook her head sympathetically. 'What a waste.'

Lucy was pleading with her. She clutched Nikki's arm, close to tears. 'Oh, please, Nikki. Ring them up for me. Please.'

Nikki feigned reluctance. She had just had an idea. 'But what if I get into trouble?'

'You won't.'

Nikki pretended to consider this. 'You promise you won't tell anyone?'

'I promise. I promise.'

Nikki thought some more. She still looked quite doubtful about what she was being asked to do. 'All right,' she said, moving to the telephone.

Nikki made the telephone call. She told the girl at the television station that her name was Lucy Robinson, then listened intently to the instructions she was given. 'Can I wear your pink top and blue eye shadow?' Lucy asked her excitedly when she had finished.

'Lucy, it's not going to work,' Nikki said with a sigh.

'But it's all arranged. You've made the phone call. Do you want some chocolate milk?'

Nikki helped Lucy make the drinks. Lucy's grandmother and father had gone to bed. It was quite late. Lucy spoke dreamily. 'Can you imagine it? Tomorrow night I'll be out with Rolf Pertwee. He might like me a real lot, and ask me to go surf-skiing with him. He's so sweet.'

Nikki looked at her doubtfully. 'He'll take one look at you and send you home.'

'He will not.' Lucy stamped her foot. 'Rolf's not like that.'

'Your Dad will never let you go.'

But Lucy had an answer for that, too. 'I'll tell him I'm going over to Sarah's to do my homework.'

'Oh yes? All dressed up in high heels and eye shadow?'

That stumped her. Her face clouded. 'Well, I won.' Her voice took on a high, querulous tone. 'He's *expecting* me to come.'

Nikki was developing her idea. 'Well . . . yes,' she said slowly. 'It *is* a bit of a waste, especially when it's all arranged. He'll think you didn't want to meet him.'

'But I do!'

Nikki went on. 'But if someone you knew went in your place, she could tell Rolf all about you.'

'Who?' Lucy stared at her with growing suspicion. She made a shrewd guess. 'You rat. That's what *you* wanted.'

'Sssh. I didn't.'

'You did so.'

'Well, it's much better than nothing, isn't it?' Nikki said with a shrug. 'I like him as much as you do.'

'You do not.' Lucy was outraged. 'I'm going to tell Dad.'

'Then you'll have to tell him you lied,' Lucy said deliberately. 'And that you were going to sneak out.'

'It's not fair.'

'I could get you his autograph,' Nikki suggested.

'I've already got it.'

Nikki tried to think of what else she could offer as a bribe. A sly gleam appeared in Lucy's eyes. 'How about next week's pocket money?'

Nikki protested. 'But, Lucy, I'll need it.'

'Well, if you don't want to go.' Lucy shrugged expressively and left the rest unsaid.

It was an enormous price to pay – and Lucy knew it only too well. Realising she had no choice, Nikki gave in. 'All right then.'

'Lucky thing,' Lucy said with a wistful expression.

It was sheer extortion, of course, but Nikki was happy. She had just got what she wanted without too much trouble otherwise. She began to dream about herself and Rolf Pertwee, who would no doubt find her extremely interesting, a fun person to be with. Naturally he would want to see her again. Surf-skiing, running along the sand. She stopped dreaming. 'But remember,' she said to Lucy with some urgency, 'it's our secret – okay?'

Lucy had no choice but to accept this. Solemnly, they clinked their glasses.

But secret or not, Nikki was bursting to tell someone about her date with the Iron Man that night. She chose Sue Parker, who was one of her best friends at school, and on whom she felt she could rely to keep it to herself. She sought her out during the morning break.

'Sue, if I tell you something, will you promise not to tell anyone?'

'Tell me what?'

'You've got to promise.'

'Okay. What?'

'I've got a date with Rolf Pertwee tonight.'

'You?' Sue gaped at her. They had been talking about it earlier. Someone had said it was a local girl whose name had been drawn from the revolving barrel. Someone else had said it was Lucy Robinson, Scott Robinson's little sister. There had been general expressions of envy that she could be so lucky. 'You're kidding. How come?'

'Well, Scott's sister really *did* win,' Nikki informed her friend. 'But she can't go because she's too young.' She smiled triumphantly. 'She said I could go instead.'

Nikki was feeling proud; now the girls would envy *her*. Then she remembered it was supposed to be a secret. Sue was staring at her in admiration. 'Why didn't you say?'

'I don't know,' Nikki replied offhandedly. 'No reason, I guess.'

'You're weird.' She shook her head in puzzlement. 'What are you going to wear?'

'I don't know yet.

'I'd die.' Sue's eyes were gleaming with envy. 'I mean, what will you say to him?'

'I'll think of something.' The conversation would simply *flow*. They would have so much in common.

'He's cute,' Sue pronounced. 'Do you think you'll be able to contain yourself?'

'Don't be silly, Sue.' Of course she would; she would handle it in a graceful and worldly way. She wasn't just some silly schoolgirl who would find herself tongue-tied in the Presence. 'It's only dinner. And besides, he's a perfect gentleman.'

'Who's pretty hot,' Sue observed. 'I bet Mike will go mental.'

Mike? Nikki suddenly felt a little deflated. Why did she have to bring in Mike Young on this day of days? It wasn't as if she and Mike were in any real sense of the word *serious*. Oh, they had been going together for some time now; they'd had their fights and pinpricking jealousies; times, such as now, when they didn't speak – but Mike could hardly be put in the same class as Iron Man Rolf Pertwee. Mike was young and immature. He didn't surf-ski or go sprinting across the sand in the grey, pink-edged light of dawn. 'It's got nothing to do with Mike,' she said a little resentfully.

'You mean,' Sue's eyes widened, 'you haven't told him yet?'

No, she hadn't; nor did she wish him to find out. Nikki shook her head. 'And don't forget,' she said. 'You promised not to tell anyone.'

She had to get ready for her big date. She had to look sophisticated. She combed her hair in a hundred different ways – there was no time to go to a hairdresser, and even if there were, suspicions would be aroused.

She told her aunt that she and a friend from school were hoping to do some studying together that evening. She didn't feel at all easy about having to lie. 'Yes, that'll be fine,' Helen Daniels said. 'Don't be late.'

That was settled. Scott came home. 'I heard a funny rumour today at school,' he said. 'Something about Lucy winning a date with Rolf Pertwee. On that show – "Date with a Star".'

'It must have been someone with the same name,' Nikki said quickly, with a warning glance at Lucy who was looking uneasy.

Nikki felt as if she were walking a tightrope. She wasn't free yet. 'What's in the bag?' Jim Robinson asked as she was about to leave the house. 'You're not staying overnight, are you?'

The bag contained her best dress. 'Oh, just some reference books.'

'Well, study hard,' Helen advised her.

'Do you want me to pick you up later?' Jim queried.

'No, it's all right,' Nikki replied quickly. 'Karen's dad will bring me home. Bye.'

'Bye.'

Finally, she was free. She had told lies, and didn't feel good about that – but now she was free to meet the man who set the hearts of all her school friends a-flutter. She wished it wasn't necessary to keep it a secret.

Lucy followed her to the door. 'You can't meet Rolf Pertwee dressed in those old clothes,' she said reproachfully. 'You look so daggy.'

They were on the front porch. Nikki kept her voice low. 'My good dress is in the bag, silly.'

'Oh, and where are you going to get changed?'

'In the ladies' room at the Regal Hotel.'

'I wish I were going,' Lucy said with a wistful sigh.

'I'll tell you all about tonight,' Nikki said, 'when I get back. Now I've got to go. Otherwise I'll be late. Wish me luck.'

The Regal Hotel was new and glittering, and had fifty floors. It was here that Nikki was having dinner with Rolf Pertwee. The woman to whom she had spoken on the telephone, and who was supposed to be organising it all, had arranged to meet her in the lobby. She was late. Nikki was very nervous. She was trembling like a leaf. In the ladies' room she had changed into her best dress and put on some make-up, but she still hadn't been satisfied when she regarded herself in the mirror. She had felt there was nothing she could do to make herself look just right for Rolf Pertwee. She felt so inadequate, so small, so exposed – particularly when the superbly groomed woman with the long blonde hair loomed up out of nowhere and said, with an encouraging smile. 'You must be Lucy.'

Nikki nodded shyly. The woman introduced herself. 'I'm Moira Matthews. I'm Rolf Pertwee's agent. He should be along in just a minute. You're not nervous, are you?' She sailed on without waiting for a reply. 'Just relax and enjoy yourself. That's all he ever asks of people. He's really a very nice guy. Ah, there he is now.'

Across the lobby the lift doors had just opened to bring forth an apparition who, lithely, and athletically, was striding towards them. Nikki was transfixed. She just stared at him with her mouth open. He was smiling. He came up to them. 'Hi, Moira.'

'This is Lucy,' Moira told him. 'Lucy, this is Rolf Pertwee.'

As if she didn't already know. As if those wonderful blue eyes that were smiling so warmly into her own could have belonged to anyone else. 'Hi.'

He kissed her perfunctorily on the cheek. Nikki's flesh tingled. 'Pretty name for a pretty girl,' Rolf said. He glanced in the direction of the hotel restaurant and rubbed his hands briskly together. 'Well, folks, what do you say? Shall we eat?'

Surely, it had to be a dream. Sooner or later, she would awake with a feeling of sadness as the images faded behind the reality of her own room and the knowledge that she soon must get ready for school. But here she was, in the restaurant of the Regal Hotel, and Rolf Pertwee was seated opposite her. The service was quick and silent. People in other parts of the restaurant, recognising Rolf, surreptitiously pointed him out to each other. There was soft music and asparagus, veal and baby carrots. Rolf sipped mineral water and talked about himself – and it wasn't long before Nikki's nervousness evaporated and she was feeling quite at ease.

'It's getting late,' Moira said finally. 'Don't forget

you have a photographic session in the morning.'

'Oh yes.' Rolf looked disappointed.

He hadn't eaten much. He had explained to Nikki that he was in training. He had pressed her to have some dessert when she hesitated. 'You won this dinner,' he had told her, 'so you get the works. Anything you like.'

Now, when Moira said, 'early to bed, early to rise – that's the rule, I'm afraid', it was Nikki's turn to look disappointed. The evening had gone so quickly. Somehow, she felt cheated. The dinner had been excellent, of course, but, in a way, she had expected something more. She didn't know what. Perhaps they could have gone on somewhere. A date was a date, after all.

'I'm sorry, Lucy,' Rolf said, rising to his feet. 'It's been a great dinner, but I really must go.'

Nikki had just finished her coffee. She stood up as well. 'It's quite all right, really,' she said bravely. 'I've had a ball.'

'So have I.'

Suddenly, a light flashed. Startled and momentarily blinded, Nikki gasped. 'Hey,' Moira cried. Nikki blinked as Rolf moved around the table to stand by her side. He placed his arm around her shoulder. Nikki could make out the man with the camera. There was another flash and she was briefly blinded again.

'Just publicity,' Rolf explained, a third flash delayed Nikki's efforts to focus. 'You get used to it after a while.'

Her photograph had been taken with the famous Rolf Pertwee! He had had his arm around her. As soon as she realised this, Nikki began to feel mightily important. Despite the quickness with which it had seemed to pass, the night had been a huge success after all. She had no right to feel disappointed.

'Come on, tell me. What happened?' Sue Parker was anxious for news.

'Ah,' Nikki sighed. It had been a long time before she had finally fallen asleep, and now here she was, back again at school. Yes, it could well have been a dream. 'Well, there's not much to say, really, other than it was the most wonderful, terrific, fabulous, probably the best night I've ever had in my whole life.'

Sue rolled her eyes. 'Why couldn't it have been me?'

Having come so far, Nikki gave in to the temptation to elaborate a little. It wouldn't do any harm, she thought. 'As a matter of fact,' she said confidentially, 'Rolf has, ah, asked me to give him a call next week. He thought we might see a movie together.'

'Really?' Sue was clearly impressed.

'Uh-huh.'

'He must really like you.'

Nikki dismissed this with a rather airy wave of her hand. 'Rolf and I have a lot in common.'

'Lucky dog.'

Nikki was suddenly uncomfortable. Perhaps she had gone far enough. 'Well, you know how it is,' she said. 'Sometimes two people just hit it off. It's chemistry, I suppose.'

It might have been all right if it had been left like that. But when the photograph of her and Iron Man Rolf Pertwee appeared in one of the evening tabloids under the glaring headline, 'New Teenage Love for Rolf Pertwee', Nikki knew she was in for a tough time.

'I'm still waiting for an explanation, young lady,' Helen Daniels demanded.

The newspaper was spread out on the kitchen table, the offending photograph and headline uppermost. Nikki had already tried to explain. 'I told you,' she said miserably. 'Lucy won the date, but she was too young to go. I went instead. I used her name. That's all there was to it, Aunt Helen.'

'You lied to us, Nikki,' Helen said angrily. 'You went out alone on a date, without our permission.'

'But nothing happened,' Nikki protested. 'That picture is only a publicity stunt.'

Helen looked at her grimly. 'I'll still have to speak to Jim about this. And, in the meantime, there'll be no more nights out.'

Nikki was more worried about what Mike's reaction would be. She was sure he would have seen the photograph. If he hadn't, someone was bound to have pointed it out to him. She felt she owed him an explanation.

He was home. He glowered at her – he had seen the paper. In fact, the paper was open in front of him. He had drawn a pair of devil's horns on Rolf Pertwee's head, and a beard. Seeing this, Nikki tried to make light of it. 'Well, that's certainly an improvement on the real thing.'

'Why did you go out with him then?'

'Because I'm stupid,' she replied with a nervous smile. 'He's a big star. I thought it would be fun.'

'Sue Parker told me what a fun time you had.'

Sheeeesh! Sue Parker, and her big mouth. Nikki Dennison and *her* big mouth. 'Oh Mike, it's not true.'

'How do I know you're not lying?'

'You have to believe me, Mike,' Nikki cried. 'Nothing happened between Rolf and me. He's just a nice guy, that's all.'

Mike's finger jabbed viciously down on the newspaper photograph of a smiling couple beneath a headline. 'You look as though you're having a pretty terrific time to me.'

'Can't we just forget it.'

His lips curled in contempt. His eyes were hard. 'Nikki, why don't you rack off,' he said in a low voice. 'I don't want to see you again.'

'Mike!'

'I mean it this time, Nikki. I've had enough. This is the last time you've made a fool of me.'

It was a relationship that until now had been fairly uneven; it had just entered a particularly rocky patch.

Eight

The 'For Sale' sign had been taken from in front of the house opposite. Clive Gibbons conjectured on who the new owner might be. 'Probably some stunning young lady who needs someone to take her around,' he said hopefully.

'I'm glad someone's moving in at last,' Daphne remarked. 'I hate empty houses. They give me the creeps.'

Early on Sunday morning, the traditional calm of Ramsay Street was rudely shattered by the arrival of a removal van which pulled up outside number nineteen. Even after it had pulled up, its radio continued to blare. The sound rocked up and down the street. It blasted and destroyed anyone's hopes of having a lie-in on this day of rest.

'What's that row?' Clive demanded sleepily.

'I don't know,' Daphne said, pouring herself a glass of orange juice. 'It's probably just someone testing their stereo.'

'At this time on a Sundary morning?' Clive looked up as Mike came into the kitchen with the morning newspaper. 'What's going on out there?'

'New people moving in across the street,' Mike told him.

Clive brightened. He still had hopes that his life was about to be drastically changed somehow by the arrival of the new people. Kindred souls on the loose and looking for a place to settle. Noisy, though, on a Sunday morning. 'I think I'll get tidied up then go over and welcome them.' The genial and talented Clive Gibbons at your service, Madam, and if there's anything...

'Clive, don't be a stickybeak.'

'I'm not.' He looked at Daphne blandly. 'Remember when *I* moved in?'

Daphne sipped her juice. She had moved into Clive's house after her break-up with Des Clarke. Mike Young had moved after he had left home. There was plenty of room – and one thing Clive didn't like was to be alone in any house. 'I remember,' Daphne said drily.

And Clive remembered. 'It wasn't a very friendly reception. People peeking through their fences. Max hammering on the door.'

'What did you expect when you were parading around in a gorilla suit?'

Ah, the old gorillagram days. 'That's beside the point. The main thing is to offer the hand of friendship.'

'You mean stickybeak.'

'I'm going over now,' Clive said to Mike. 'Are you coming?'

Mike nodded. 'Sure.'

After he had made himself presentable, combing his hair and eyebrows, brushing his teeth and washing his face, Clive led the way across the street. He stood and watched the two removal men carrying furniture into the house, then looked around for a sign of the owner. 'Good morning,' he greeted the two men as they returned to the van for another load. He had to raise his voice a little to make himself heard above the radio. 'Have the new owners arrived yet?'

One of the men jerked his thumb back in the direction of the house. 'In there.'

The second man pulled a face. 'I should have stayed home with the Missus.'

What did he mean by that? Clive looked at Mike with raised eyebrows. Mike looked helplessly back at him. Scott Robinson joined them. 'What's going on?' he asked.

'New neighbours,' Mike informed him.

'That's right,' Clive said. 'We're just going to welcome them to the street.'

Then, as they were still looking around for the new owners, a bundle of enraged energy suddenly erupted on the scene. 'Turn that flamin' row off!' it bellowed. 'Haven't you got any respect for people's peace and quiet.'

The two removal men were just emerging from the back of the van, each of them carrying a tea chest. They stopped, and looked with marked curiosity at the newcomer. 'What are you doin' – playin' the radio flat out. Are ya deaf or somethin'?'

Tom Ramsay's face was mottled and contorted in rage. His fists were clenched and he was bouncing up and down on the balls of his feet. Max had gone to Queensland, and his brother had arrived from there. Birds of a feather, Clive had thought when he first encountered Tom. It seemed there would always be a troublesome and belligerent Ramsay in the street that bore the family name.

'Look, mate,' the first removal man said. 'We always have music. It's relaxing.'

'Well, it's not relaxin' *me.*'

'Listen, mate.' The man regarded him stolidly. 'We've got to have music.' Carefully, he placed his tea chest on the van's lowered tailboard. He was a rather large man. 'It's part of the terms and conditions of our employment. Now, if you don't like it, you can complain to the owner.'

'I will!' Tom shouted. 'But I'm going to shut off that row first.' He began to storm towards the cabin of the van. 'Because I can't hear myself think.'

'Hey, sport.' Jumping down from the tailboard, the removal man headed after him. 'You leave that radio alone.' Clive tried to restrain him. The man shook him off. 'Stand aside, sonny,' he growled threateningly.

'Hang on, mate.'

The second removal man by now had joined the chase. He grabbed Tom's arm just as Tom managed to switch off the radio. 'Oi, you leave that radio alone.' He dragged Tom away from the van.

'What is this?' an all-too-familiar voice demanded. 'A riot on my own doorstep? Break it up immediately, or I'll call the police.' The new owner had just emerged from the house.

Everyone froze. They stared. Tom swore. 'Mrs Mangel,' he groaned. 'That's *all* I need.'

Yes, it was Mrs Mangel who was standing there with her arms folded, surveying the incredulous assembly with a forbidding expression. 'No wonder they had so much difficulty in selling this house,' she said. Scott and Mike edged away. Clive's mouth had fallen open. Mrs Mangel shook her head. 'This street leaves a lot to be desired,' she pronounced imperiously.

'It was all right till this morning,' Tom muttered.

Mrs Mangel bore down on him. 'What was that, Mr Ramsay?'

This time Tom spoke very clearly. 'I said it was all right till this morning.' He gestured in disgust. 'Ah, to hell with it. I need some breakfast.' He stomped back towards the Ramsay house.

'I'll be keeping an eye on you, Tom Ramsay,' Mrs Mangel called sharply after him. Then seeing that the removal men were just gaping at her and not doing anything, she rounded on them. 'I'm not paying your exorbitant rates just to leave my furniture lying around in the open.'

The two men nodded to each other, then picking up the tea chests, carried them up the path to the house.

Mrs Mangel turned her ferocious glare on to Clive. He had come to welcome the new arrival, and had rehearsed a little speech. He decided not to waste it. He gave her one of his sincere smiles. 'On behalf of all the residents of Ramsay Street,' he said warmly, 'I would like to welcome you here. And if there's anything I can do,' he pointed to his house, 'I live just over there. So please,' he spoke with an effort now, 'pop in any time.'

Mrs Mangel's eyes narrowed dubiously. 'All right then,' she said crisply. 'I'll be over in about five minutes for a cup of tea.'

Dejectedly, with the feeling that all the wind had been taken from his sails, Clive stared after her as she marched back up the path to her front door.

She was true to her word. Within five minutes, she was casting an eagle eye around Clive's living room. In the kitchen, Clive and Daphne were preparing the tea. 'Are you crazy?' Daphne hissed. 'Why did you invite her here?'

'I didn't exactly invite her,' Clive whispered back. 'Besides, we might as well try and be friendly with the woman. After all, we have to live in the same street as her.'

'It's very rude to whisper, you know,' Mrs Mangel said suddenly and distinctly behind them. Daphne and Clive exchanged a quick, guilty glance before Clive picked up the tray with the tea things on it and carried it into the living room.

Mrs Mangel admired the tea cups which Clive hadn't thought of as being anything special. 'I think they do such clever things with imitation china nowadays,' she said sweetly, then nodded to the teapot. 'I hope the tea has had time to draw properly.'

Clive apologised for the fact that there was no cake. Daphne poured the tea, then straightened. 'If you'll excuse me, Mrs Mangel,' she said. 'I have a few things to do.' She smiled at Clive, who glowered back at her. Such a great help *she* was.

'Well,' Mrs Mangel said comfortably after Daphne had gone, 'I understand you were once a doctor.'

'It was a long time ago,' Clive murmured uncomfortably.

Mrs Mangel nodded. 'The healing hand.'

'One facet, Mrs Mangel, of a multi-faceted existence.' Clive rather liked the sound of that.

'I've never been one to complain, you know.' Mrs Mangel sipped her tea, winced a little, then put the cup down on its saucer. 'Even though life hasn't treated me very well, I've always managed to look on the bright side of things. It's the only way.'

'Ride with the punches,' Clive said sagely. 'Oh yes,

how right you are. Positive thinking. Don't let the bast . . .'

'And my legs aren't what they used to be.'

'Oh? That's a shame. You should see a doctor.'

Mrs Mangel sighed. 'You have no idea how many doctors I've seen already. They don't know what's wrong with me. I'm a difficult case, you see. Specialists, too. They just shake their heads.'

Clive had already guessed what was coming. 'I suppose they do,' he said with compassion.

'And the prices they charge. Oh, it's quite monstrous.'

Ah. Clive was treading warily by now. 'I agree,' he said sympathetically.

Mrs Mangel looked speculatively at her teacup. Clive wondered what Daphne was doing. 'It's no wonder I'm struggling while they – they live in *mansions*.'

'It's a crying shame,' Clive observed.

'Of course there are some doctors who still remember their – their oath of hypocrisy.'

Oh, you *cunning* one, Clive thought. Oh, you sly old thing. 'Oh, I'm sure there must be hundreds.'

'But none of them . . . Ah . . . Um . . . Close by . . .' She gave him a conspiratorial smile. 'Doctor.'

'I no longer practice, Mrs Mangel. I'm still licensed, of course, but –'

'And it cost us little people a fortune to put you through medical school.' A smalll note of reproach had crept into her voice.

'Actually, my father paid for it,' Clive pointed out to her.

'It's the same difference,' Mrs Mangel said smugly.

Suddenly, Clive felt trapped. 'Just what exactly *is* the problem, Mrs Mangel?'

Now she was a little coy. 'Ah, I know you'll keep this . . . confidential.'

Clive was beginning to see a way out of this; there was a faint glimmer of light at the end of the tunnel. He moved out of his chair and sat down on the couch next to her. He placed his arm along the back of the couch behind her and crossed his legs. He looked very expansive and relaxed. 'I've never told anyone this, Mrs Mangel,' he said with a rather low and lewd chuckle, 'but confidential problems are a speciality of mine.'

She was sitting tensely forward on the edge of the couch. She looked at him doubtfully, then at his arm along the back of the couch. 'Perhaps I had better come back another time,' she suggested.

Clive laughed, then laid his hand on her arm. She flinched. 'Everyone panics – it's a normal reaction. So now. Why don't you pop into the bedroom and take off your clothes?'

'I beg your pardon?'

'I said . . .'

'I heard what you said.' Mrs Mangel sprang to her feet.

Clive smiled reassuringly up at her. Mrs Mangel's face had suddenly become very pinched. 'Well, I *do* have to examine you if we are to obtain an accurate diagnosis.'

Mrs Mangel began to head for the front door. 'You're *not* getting your hands on me, young man,' she cried indignantly.

Clive followed her into the hall. 'Please, Mrs Mangel, I'm only here to serve.'

Mrs Mangel wrenched open the front door. She turned and fixed him with an eye that brooked no compromise. 'It's no *wonder* you're not practising.

You're nothing but a . . . but a . . . a sex maniac.'

'A sex . . .'

Vigorously, Mrs Mangel pulled the door closed behind her. Clive gleefully rubbed his hands together and returned to the living room where the tea was getting cold. He was very pleased with the outcome of that little episode. Mrs Mangel wouldn't be around again in a hurry.

Nine

Helen Daniels was a little worried about old Mrs York. She didn't look well, and she was much thinner than she had been. And then there was that dizzy turn she had had just as she was turning into her front gate. Helen hadn't liked the look of it at all.

Helen was on her way home from the shops. Seeing Mrs York walking along the street ahead of her, she caught up with the old woman.

'Oh, Helen.' Mrs York looked mildly startled to see her. Then she smiled and indicated Helen's shopping bags. 'You seem to have quite a load there.'

'Tell that to my family,' Helen said with a laugh. 'They'll demolish the lot in a day or two, and then insist on more. It's like feeding time at the zoo.'

'Still, a nice friendly zoo,' Mrs York said a little ruefully.

'I'm glad you feel that way because you'll probably have a visit from some of the animals tonight.'

'Oh?'

'They're collecting for a school charity,' Helen explained. 'And I'm afraid you've been, er, targeted as a soft touch.'

If Mrs York hesitated at that point, it was barely perceptible. Helen wasn't sure, in fact, if it had been there. It was just an impression she had. Then Mrs York was saying, quite brightly, 'Oh, I don't mind. I'd be happy to contribute.'

They had just reached the house where Mrs York had been living alone since the death of her husband. Mrs York was taking her mail out of the letter box when suddenly she gasped, and dropping the letters, staggered a little before clutching the letter-box for support.

'Mrs York, are you all right?'

The old woman was taking deep breaths. She nodded. 'Yes, thank you. Just a dizzy turn. I get them now and again. Nothing serious.'

Helen picked up the letters from the footpath and handed them to her. 'Are you sure?'

Mrs York gave her a wan smile. 'I'm afraid I have to accept this sort of thing at my age.' She was breathing more easily now.

Despite these reassurances, Helen wasn't totally convinced. She picked up Mrs York's bag from where it had fallen. 'Thank you.' Mrs York nodded to the bag. 'Daphne's been saving these for me. Leftovers from the coffee shop. Stale buns, that sort of thing for the animals I feed. I don't like to see them go hungry.'

Helen was still worried. 'Mrs York, perhaps you'd like to come and have dinner with us tonight,' she offered impulsively.

'No. No, thank you.' The old woman appeared momentarily disconcerted. 'I already have a chicken marinading. It's just a matter of putting it in the oven.'

'I just thought I might save you the trouble of cooking.'

'That's very kind of you,' the old woman said with a smile. 'Some other time, perhaps.'

'Of course.'

Helen watched as she moved rather carefully up the path to her front door. She still wasn't convinced that everything was really all right.

She mentioned her misgivings to Jim that evening. 'I think she's very lonely,' she said.

'Yes, and too proud to admit it by the sound of things,' he observed.

'Still, I must find a way of dropping in on her more often,' Helen said thoughtfully. 'She's very defensive, and it might be difficult. But I should still try.'

When Nikki came home the following evening she complained that she had only managed to collect some small change from Mrs York when she and the others had called on her. Even then they had been lucky to find her, working in her garden, because on the two occasions they had knocked on her front door before then, there had been no response. Helen was surprised. Mrs York had always been a generous woman with her money in the past. 'That doesn't sound like the Annabelle York I know,' she said.

'Perhaps she's tired of being hit for money all the time,' Scott suggested.

Helen frowned at her grandson. 'Mrs York is one of the most charitable women I know,' she said, a little tersely. 'She has *always* given to charities. If she only gave you a dollar, or whatever it was, there must have been a very good reason for it.'

'Like what?' Nikki queried.

Helen didn't know. All she did know was that things were not as they should be as far as Mrs York was concerned.

'Maybe she's going a bit, you know, loopy or something,' Scott said thoughtfully.

'Soctt!'

About a week later, Madge Mitchell dropped in to see Helen. There was something on her mind. She seemed a little evasive. 'I wanted to see you,' she began, 'because being a Community Justice Counsellor I thought you might be able to give me some advice.'

'Well, I'll try.'

'You see, there's this woman I know. Now, before her husband died, the two of them were really quite comfortably off. But, since then she's been selling things off just to make ends meet. In fact, I think she goes without food just to keep up appearances.'

'But isn't she on the pension?' Helen asked.

'No. She sees that as charity.'

'Well, there are various community care projects for which she's most probably eligible,' Helen said. 'There's Meals on Wheels, for instance.'

'No. Oh no.'

Helen looked at her quizzically. 'Too proud?'

Madge nodded emphatically. 'Far too proud.'

Helen thought for a monent. 'If she's a local person, I could have a word with her.'

'She's not local,' Madge said quickly.

'I see.' Helen stood up. 'Look, I've got some pamphlets in my room. There might be some useful information in them.'

'That's much appreciated, Helen.'

Neither of them were aware then that Nikki, just beyond the living room doorway, had heard most of this conversation.

In the morning, Lucy asked for a larger school lunch than usual. 'Are you sure you can eat all that?' Helen queried in some surprise.

'Of course I can. I could probably eat even more than that.'

'Don't tell me you're turning into a horse, Lucy,' Jim said.

'I'm a growing girl,' she told him. 'I have to eat lots.'

'All right.' Helen handed her the lunch box. 'I made it, so just make sure you eat it.'

When Lucy arrived home after school that afternoon, Helen asked her if she had eaten all her lunch. 'Not exactly,' Lucy replied uncomfortably.

'What do you mean, not exactly?'

'I'm sorry.' Lucy was looking a little guilty. 'I made it up when I said I was hungry.' She took a deep breath. 'I gave the extra lunch to Mrs York.'

'Good heavens.' Helen stared at her grand-daughter in surprise. 'Why would you do that?'

Lucy spoke hesitantly. 'Well, you know when Mrs Mitchell was talking to you, and she was talking about an old lady who didn't have enough to eat?'

Helen was trying to remember what Madge *had* said. She hadn't given it a great deal of thought at the time. 'Hmm?'

'That was Mrs York.'

Helen was shocked to hear it. 'Darling, are you sure? How do you know it *was* Mrs York she was talking about? I'm sure she mentioned no names.'

'It was Mrs York,' Lucy stated. 'Nikki heard you talking. She told us. It could *only* be Mrs York you were talking about. She's an old lady. She hasn't got any money or food, or anything.'

Helen's shock was replaced by concern. She had no *idea*. Mrs York had said nothing, had intimated nothing. 'Oh, I should go over and see if there's anything I can do.'

'You can't,' Lucy said unhappily. 'She said she didn't want any of my sandwiches. And she didn't want any charity or help from anyone. She was quite angry.'

Of course Mrs York had her pride, but this was ridiculous. 'That makes it difficult,' Helen murmured.

'Why is she being like this, Gran?' Lucy wanted to know.

'It's pride, darling,' Helen told her. Pride pure and simple. 'Some people just can't admit that they need help.'

Lucy was bewildered. 'But you and Dad help me all the time. And Mrs York has helped lots of people – so she should let people help *her*, shouldn't she?'

If it only were as simple as that. 'I'm afraid she has the right to say no if she wants to,' Helen said. 'And that means no more taking sandwiches to her.'

As Helen learnt later from Madge Mitchell, Mrs York's condition would have remained unknown if Tom Ramsay hadn't been called to the house to fix a broken water pipe. Mrs York had tried to cope with it herself, but it had been too much for her. there had been water everywhere. Mrs York had been desperate. She had been struggling with a bucket and a mop.

After he had fixed the pipe, Tom had noticed something peculiar about the house. It had taken him a few moments, Madge said, to realise what it was. Then it had come to him that there was hardly any furniture in the house. The walls were bare, and there were no carpets on the floor. 'Strike me purple,' he had said in astonishment.

Mrs York had spun him some story about a robbery. All her fine paintings had been taken, and just about everything she had. She had said something about waiting for the insurance people to replace it all, but she hadn't been convincing. Tom had thought it was strange that he had not heard anything about a robbery in the street. Mrs York had become quite upset. Was he doubting her word? Of course not, he had said.

And Madge had also thought it was strange. Everyone would have known about it if there had been a robbery in the street. Madge had decided to offer Mrs York some of her old furniture which she had stored in the garage.

Helen was appalled. Something definitely had to be done. 'Look, I'll go and see her in the morning,' she said. 'I've known her a fair while. Perhaps I can persuade her.'

Madge was looking at her worriedly. 'I really think it's more urgent than that, Helen. I have a feeling that she doesn't have anything to eat for tonight.'

Helen pushed her chair back and stood up. 'In that case I'd better go now,' she said.

'It was so sad,' she told Helen as they sat over a cup of tea. 'There she was, in this house that had absolutely nothing in it. She was very embarrassed. She insisted on making tea. The biscuits were very old. She talked about the robbery – and honestly, Helen, you could see that there was something wrong there. She did say something, though,' Madge went on with a small frown. 'She was talking about her husband and how he had been dead for fifteen years. She showed me his photograph. She said something about letting him down. I asked her how, and she said about having to let everything in the house go. Then she clammed up. And then I knew for certain that there hadn't been a robbery. I came right out with it, and told her, and in the end she broke down and admitted it. There hadn't been a robbery at all, but she had been forced to sell everything. Her husband had been retired early on a reduced pension, and after he died, there was the inflation.' Madge shook her head sorrowfully. 'Oh Helen, it's just not fair. She was always helping people in the past – and now *she* needs help. I took some food around to her this morning, and she wouldn't accept it. She's been living all this time on scraps and leftovers. There's just her and the little dog of hers. She's absolutely devoted to it. She probably gives it more food than she has herself.'

But when she arrived at Mrs York's house with a basket of food and rang the front door bell, there was no response. She tried again; she tried a number of times. Nor was there any response when she tried the back door. Thinking that the old lady might be asleep, she decided to try again in the morning.

But in the morning, there was still no response from inside the house. Inside, Helen could hear the dog whimpering, then barking. Seeing Clive Gibbons emerge from his own front door, she called to him. 'Clive, I think there's something wrong here.'

They tried both doors. They were locked. 'I think you're right,' Clive said.

'Perhaps we should call the police.'

'I'll try the windows.' Clive moved to one of the front windows.

He was still trying to force it when Mrs Mangel arrived on the scene. 'What do you think you're doing?' she demanded.

Helen swung to face her. 'Mrs Mangel, we're worried

about Mrs York. Please don't interfere.'

Having been unable to force the window, Clive was now trying to peer through it. Inside, the dog was barking more frantically. 'Why is that dog barking like that?' Mrs Mangel asked in a querulous tone.

Clive was moving to the other window. 'That's what we're trying to find out.'

When he had no luck with that window, Clive said he would see if he had more success at the back of the house. 'I don't think you should do that,' Mrs Mangel said primly. 'That's against the law.'

They ignored her. As Clive disappeared around the side of the house, Helen began to knock urgently on the front door. 'Mrs York?' she cried. 'Mrs York! Is anyone there?'

The dog was there. It was still yelping and barking. Helen followed Clive to the rear of the house. Mrs Mangel was already there. 'You're not going to break in?' she exclaimed in a horrified voice as Clive managed to open one of the windows. 'I told you – it's against the law.'

Clive had hoisted himself up onto the sill. 'Shut up, Mrs Mangel,' he growled over his shoulder as he clambered into the room beyond.

A moment later, he opened the back door. His expression was grim. Helen hurried past him into the house, then stopped abruptly when she saw Mrs York lying on the floor. 'Get an ambulance,' Clive ordered, dropping to his knees beside the unconscious woman to make a quick examination of her.

Helen glanced at Mrs Mangel who had followed her inside. 'Would you do that? You'd better go next door. I have a feeling the phone here has been cut off.'

The dog, lying on the floor beside its mistress, was looking up at them with sorrowful eyes. Its tail lifted once then fell again; it whimpered softly. Clive checked Mrs York's pulse rate, her eyes, and her breathing. He pinched her skin to establish if there were any dehydration. Helen, staring down at her, kept shaking her head. 'The poor woman,' she breathed.

Mrs Mangel still hadn't moved. 'Is she dead?'

'No.' Clive glanced up at Helen. 'Get me some water.'

Helen turned towards the kitchen. She frowned at Mrs Mangel. 'I thought I asked you to get an ambulance?'

Mrs Mangel was looking around the room. 'There's hardly any furniture,' she noted in surprise. 'Oh dear.' Her face fell. 'It must have been stolen. Yes, that's what happened. The poor woman has been bashed and robbed.' She was aghast.

On the floor, Mrs York groaned. 'Mrs York?' Clive said urgently. 'Are you okay?' Helen came back with a glass of water. She handed it to Clive who was cradling Mrs York's head in his arm. 'Here, sip this,' Clive urged gently. 'It's water.'

Mrs Yorks eyes were open. She blinked rapidly a number of times as she tried to focus. 'Mrs Daniels.'

'Hello.' Helen smiled down at her.

'What, what happened?'

'I think you fainted, Mrs York,' Clive told her.

'Fainted my foot,' Mrs Mangel exclaimed in disgust. 'The poor woman has been attacked.' She bent over Mrs York. 'They've stolen all your furniture, my dear.'

'Furniture?' There was incomprehension in the old woman's eyes. 'What furniture?'

'I think you should let us take you to a hospital,' Clive

said.

'Hospital?' Mrs York shook her head and struggled to sit upright. 'I couldn't go to hospital. It was just a silly faint.'

'Please. Just relax.'

Helen was still staring down at her. 'Mrs York, when did you last have a meal?' she asked quietly.

'A meal?' Mrs York looked blank.

'Well, let's get you to hospital, and we can sort things out from there.'

'But, Billy. What about Billy? I can't leave him.' Billy's tail lifted then fell again.

'I'll look after Billy,' Helen promised her.

Mrs York sighed. 'Poor Billy. He's all I've got now.'

As soon as she was able to receive visitors, Helen visited her in her hospital room. She was sitting up in her bed, idly fingering her wedding ring. Helen sat beside her.

'I even thought of selling my ring,' Mrs York said wistfully. 'But that was one thing I couldn't do. It was the only thing that gave me the strength to carry on.'

Helen knew only too well how she felt. 'Yes, I remember when I lost my husband, I sat and looked at my wedding ring. I remembered the good times, and the bad.'

Mrs York looked very small beneath the hospital blankets. Her voice was almost a whisper. 'It's been fifteen years now, and I still love him.' She gave a small sad smile. 'He did everything for me. He always said I would be well looked after. And I was, until five years ago. Then it became difficult to make ends meet as the bills began mounting up. The bank was unable to help. I had to sell things. Jewellery, paintings, the furniture, until there was nothing left to sell. I became so bad that I couldn't find enough to pay for food.'

'But you could have called Meals on Wheels.'

'I thought of that," Mrs Yorks said distantly. 'But I'm a stupid old woman, Mrs Daniels. I was trying to keep up appearances, you see – and for what? I don't suppose it really matters now.'

'Mrs York.' Helen leaned forward on her chair. 'I have a friend who might be able to give you some advice. Would you mind if he came here and had a talk with you?'

'You've done enough for me already.'

'Nonsense.'

Clive Gibbons came breezily into the room. 'How are you feeling, Mrs York?'

Mrs York smiled at him. 'Oh, much better, thank you.'

'Good.' Clive came around to the foot of the bed. 'I've had a long talk with the doctor who admitted you. He says he'll do everything he can to have you up and about again as soon as possible.'

'But he doesn't have to worry,' Mrs York said with a slight frown. 'I'm really all right. If I could only go home.'

Clive shook his head. 'Not yet.'

'But it's so wrong,' the old woman protested. 'All I had was a silly fainting spell – and I'm occupying a bed that must be needed for people who are seriously ill.'

'Believe me, Mrs York,' Helen said earnestly, 'they won't keep you a minute longer than is absolutely necessary.'

Mrs York was imploring them both with her eyes. 'I really would like to go home. There are things I have to do.'

'If it's your dog you're worrying about,' Helen said, 'we'll look after him.'

'That's very kind.'

A nurse came into the room with a covered tray. Helen stood up. 'We'd better go,' she said with a glance at Clive.

As the nurse began to check her pulse, Mrs York said, 'Thank you, both of you. I'm sorry.' She closed her eyes. 'I've caused so much bother.'

Everybody began to rally around her. They brought her gifts and flowers. They made plans. 'We've just been to see Mrs York,' Scott told Helen as he and Nikki came into the house the following afternoon.

'How is she?'

'Fiercely independent. I think that about sums her up.'

'We said we're all going to help her when she comes out of hospital,' Nikki supplied. 'But I think it's going to be a bit of a battle.'

Scott nodded. 'Mike and I told her we would look after her house from now on,' he said. 'And the garden. She said she's thinking of selling the house and moving into a unit. We said we would help her move.'

'And Charlene and I said we would do her shopping,' Nikki said. 'At the market – where it's cheaper.'

Helen smiled at them fondly, and a little mistily. She was proud of them both. She was proud of all of them. She was proud of her street where such a spirit of goodwill and co-operation could so quickly make itself manifest. It was wonderful the way people could rally like this.

'It really is so incredible,' Mrs York said that evening.

'I, I didn't realise people could be so kind. And those young ones this afternoon. Do you know they even promised to help me with the shopping and about the house?'

Helen had brought her flowers. She had just put them in water. The room was already full of flowers. 'You should let them.'

'Oh, they don't want to be bothered with an old woman. They have their own lives to lead.'

'Oh Mrs York,' Helen said in a tone of mild reproach. 'If they hadn't wanted to do it, they wouldn't have offered.'

'Oh.'

Looking rather serious, Clive joined them. 'I've just been talking to Mrs York's doctor,' he informed Helen, then turned to the old woman in the bed. 'Do you mind if we discuss this?'

'I *do* want to go home, Clive,' Mrs York said with determination.

'If you book yourself out they won't accept any responsibility for you.'

Helen was surprised; this was the first she had heard of it. 'You tried to book yourself out?'

'I thought they would welcome the opportunity of having a spare bed,' Mrs York replied. 'The doctor wasn't happy, but he did say I could go home tomorrow.'

Helen was incredulous. Really, this woman and her pride. 'But you've been very ill, Mrs York. If the doctors say you shouldn't go home, then you shouldn't.'

The old woman regarded her levelly from the pillows. 'I know, Mrs Daniels. But I do miss my little house. And Billy.'

'Well, stay here tonight then,' Clive said. 'And if they

say you can go home tomorrow then I'll come and get you. Is that agreed?'

Mrs York hesitated, then nodded briefly. 'Thank you, Clive.'

They brought her home the following morning. Mrs York was obviously relieved to be back in her own house again. 'Now while we're away,' Clive instructed her, 'I want you to promise that if you feel tired, you'll go straight to bed.'

'I promise.'

'Good. I've got the key, so we can let ourselves in when we come back with the groceries.'

'Don't forget some food for Billy.'

'It's right at the top of the list.'

Before they left, Helen made her a cup of tea. 'Now is there anything else we can do for you before we go?' she asked.

Mrs York shook her head. Her eyes were moist. 'You've all been so very kind,' she said, a little tremulously. She looked around the room, then at the photographs on the mantelpiece. 'It's so nice to be back here. There are so many memories, you see.'

Helen and Clive headed for the door. 'We won't be long.

When they returned, about an hour later, the old woman was still seated in the armchair where they had left her. Her hands were resting on her lap. Beneath them was a framed photograph. She was smiling.

'We're back, Mrs York,' Clive said as Helen carried the shopping bags into the kitchen. 'Mrs York?' Helen put the groceries down on the kitchen table. 'Mrs York?' There was something in the sound of Clive's voice that triggered off an alarm in Helen. She hurried back into the other room.

As she entered the room, Clive gently placed the old woman's lifeless hand back on to her lap, on top of the framed photograph, and solemnly shook his head. The old woman looked so . . . so peaceful. Helen began to cry.